WHITE RIVER WOLVES

SLADE'S DESIRE

DAWN SULLIVAN

Published by Dawn Sullivan

Cover Design: Kari Ayasha-Cover to Cover Designs

Photographer: Mandy Hollis Photography

Models: Julio Elving and Ashley Edmund

Copyright 2016 © Author Dawn Sullivan

Language: English

For all of my wonderful readers. When I began my writing journey just over a year and a half ago, I never would have dreamed I would be where I am today. Always follow your dreams. You never know where you will end up! Thank you so much for your continued support. It means the world to me.

So, this was where they had taken his woman, he thought snidely, as he slowly tracked the activity at the White River Wolves compound from where he was hidden on a bluff just half a mile from his prey. There were several buildings throughout the large property, along with a number of houses scattered on the outskirts of the small town. Some of the buildings he could tell were apartments because of the balconies on the second and third floors, along with the open curtains showing him exactly what was inside. Another one looked like an office building sporting blinds on all of the windows, most of which were also open. He knew shifters liked the wide, open spaces. They hated being confined in any small area, which was why all of the blinds were wide open for the world to see inside. They were either very confident that their homes would not be compromised, or very stupid.

There was another large building beyond the offices that he assumed was a hospital, because he had watched a couple of people arrive for work in scrubs just over an hour ago. That one was too far away to see inside from where he lay behind a large rock, and from his angle, it was mostly blocked by an apartment building.

The compound was surrounded by a tall chain-link fence, stretching out over hundreds of acres. As far as he could tell, the fence was only on three sides of the land. It stopped where the mountains on the backside of the property began a few miles from the town. The fence seemed to be more of a deterrent than anything, because there was no way the pack would be able to watch that many acres of land closely enough that nothing could slip past them.

Readjusting his binoculars, he zoomed in on the lone wolf racing through the woods just half a mile from where he was hidden. Sunlight glistened off the huge animal's dark grey coat as he jumped lightly over a fallen tree, heading in the direction of the buildings. There was a small patch of dark brown fur on his chest, and another on his nose and the tips of his ears. Most people would see a beautiful, majestic animal, but all he saw was an abomination. Something that should never have been allowed to live in the first place.

There was another wolf with what looked like identical coloring and markings further out, running toward the first one. They had made the same loop several times since he had been there, obviously watching for any enemies that may be a threat to the people in the compound. *People,* he grunted to himself. *They weren't people. They were nothing but fucking animals. Animals that needed to be put down.*

Narrowing his eyes, he quickly swept the binoculars over the area surrounding the two wolves. No one else was in the vicinity. It was early morning, so they were probably all still in bed or eating their breakfast; oblivious to the fact that he was stalking them. Yes, that was exactly what he was doing, stalking all of the disgusting creatures in their own homes. Chuckling to himself, he put down the binoculars and picked up his sniper rifle. It would be so easy to pick them all off one by one…and he should. They had taken what belonged to him, the only thing that mattered to him, and there was no way he was going to let them get away with it. He wanted her back, and he would have her…soon.

The more he thought about how the bastards had stolen his woman from him, the angrier he became. They had taken her when he was gone, hunting down a couple of escaped women for his boss. If he'd been there, he had no doubt that she would still be with him. He owned her, dammit! He fucking *owned* her. He'd paid his boss ten thousand dollars for her, and he was taking back his possession, he didn't care who he had to kill along the way.

Fighting to calm himself, he called on his many years of training. He had been a hired assassin for over fifteen years. He knew how to look deep inside himself and connect to that part that allowed him to become unemotional and detached until the mission was complete. After several moments, he peered back through his scope and saw the wolves had almost reached each other. Making a quick decision, he pulled the trigger, laughing as the dark grey wolf fell to the forest floor. The other wolf howled loudly in distress as it quickly closed the distance between them. Pleasure coursed through him as he watched the devastation unfolding before him. Grinning in satisfaction, he slowly and methodically began taking apart the sniper rifle before putting it away in its case. Enclosing his binoculars in their bag, he picked up his belongings and walked away without a backward glance. *Soon*, he told himself, his woman would be with him again, right where she belonged.

————

AIDEN ANDREWS HOWLED LOUDLY, the sound of his heartbeat pounding in his ears as he ran swiftly to where his twin brother lay bleeding out on the ground. Fear for Xavier consumed him as Aiden watched dark red blood begin to pool on the ground beneath his body. Skidding to a stop beside the large wolf, Aiden looked around, baring his teeth in warning at any unforeseen danger, before shifting quickly. Anticipating more shots to come, he gathered Xavier in his arms and moved as quickly as possible to the buildings in the distance.

This could not be happening. He refused to lose his brother like this. Aiden was the oldest, only by a few minutes, but he still felt responsible for Xavier. Since it was just the two of them, it was his job to protect his brother. He should have been the one to take that bullet, not Xavier. Struggling to carry the two hundred pound wolf in his arms as he ran, Aiden growled deeply when he stumbled, almost dropping his precious cargo. *Not much further*, he told himself, as he rushed past the first set of apartment buildings. He just had to get to Doc Josie. She would know what to do.

Ignoring the shocked looks he received as he ran bare ass naked through the compound carrying his unconscious brother, Aiden started yelling for the doctor as soon as the hospital came into sight. Stopping briefly to adjust his hold on the wolf, he snarled when someone tried to take Xavier from him. Xavier was his brother, his responsibility, and he had failed to protect him. How the hell had someone gotten to him? They had been on patrol, and split off to do one last round before they were relieved by Sable and Charlotte. What had they missed?

"It's just me, Aiden," Chase Montgomery said soothingly, as he once again tried to take Xavier from him. "Let me help you get him to the hospital."

Aiden's nostrils flared as he breathed in his alpha's scent. "It's Xavier," Aiden rasped, clutching his brother tightly to his chest, refusing to release him to anyone, not even the pack alpha. "Someone fucking shot him, Chase," he growled, his voice full of anger and pain. "Someone shot my brother. When I find the fucker, he will wish it was me he shot instead." The last was said with purpose. Xavier was the only family Aiden had. He would do anything for him. If Xavier didn't make it...shaking his head, Aiden pushed the thought from his mind. Xavier was tough, he *would* make it. Aiden refused to believe otherwise.

Chase's eyes grew dark with fury. Reaching out, he ran a hand gently down Xavier's head before responding, "You take care of your brother, Aiden. I will find the son of a bitch who shot him." When Aiden would have protested, Chase promised, "I will keep you informed on everything I find, but right now Xavier needs you. Trust me, son, the person who shot your brother will suffer just as much, if not more, when I get my hands on him."

Nodding, his dark eyes filled with barely controlled

rage, Aiden stepped around his alpha and hurried to the hospital. Doc Josie, the physician for the White River Wolves, was waiting just inside the front doors for him. "This way, Aiden. Quickly," she ordered as she ran down the hall and through a door marked surgery.

Aiden followed, terrified because the ragged breathing from Xavier had slowed and almost stopped. After pushing his way through the swinging doors, he gently placed Xavier on the cold metal of the operating table in the middle of the room. Xavier's body shuddered as he coughed, a small trail of blood leaking from his muzzle. Blood coated the table as it seeped from the wound in his chest.

"You need to wait in the lobby area, Aiden," the doctor instructed as she donned surgical gloves. "I will come see you as soon as I know anything."

"I'm staying," Aiden snarled. He didn't want to leave Xavier. He was afraid if he did, if his brother didn't hear his voice yelling at him and pushing him to fight, Xavier wouldn't make it. And that just wasn't an option. His brother had to live.

Stopping in front of Aiden, Doc Josie glared at him. "Get the hell out of my operating room right now Aiden Andrews. I can't do my job with you looking over my shoulder. If you want your brother to have a fighting chance, you need to go, now." Aiden's body shook as he stared at his brother over her shoulder. Relenting slightly at the fear in Aiden's eyes, she told him softly, "Go, Aiden. I promise I will come get you as soon as I'm done."

"You save him, Doc," Aiden demanded through clenched teeth. "Please, you have to save him." Josie nodded, determination flaring in her eyes, as she turned and walked quickly to where Xavier lay without another word.

Stepping back toward the door, Aiden watched while the doctor and several nurses went to work on his brother. "I will find whoever did this to you, little brother," he vowed in a low, hard voice. "I promise you, I will find them."

2

Dark, it was so dark. Her body shook with pain and fear. She was so hungry. Her stomach felt horribly empty after not eating for the past two days. Unfortunately, that was normal now. The bastards waited days before feeding her, keeping her weak and unable to defend herself. She was miserable, and had been for several months. She prayed someone would save her, but they never did. Every day she would wake up in the same hell, terrified it would be her last. She couldn't die. Her sister needed her. Gypsy vowed she would live, and somehow free both Sari and herself.

Hearing the door at the top of the stairs open, Gypsy scooted back into a corner and huddled into a ball. She could not bring attention to herself. That was when they hurt her. Facing the wall, she began to rock back and forth, crying softly. Her heart raced at the sound of heavy footsteps on the stairs as her tormentors made their way down them. She screamed silently inside when they reached the bottom of the stairs and then walked in her direction. Don't let them hear you, she told herself softly. Stay quiet. Don't draw their attention. *How many more beatings would she have to survive from them? How much more suffering would she have to go through?*

The footsteps stopped at her cell, but after a few moments they moved on to the cell next to hers. Gypsy froze, listening intently. There was the sound of a key in the lock and then the cell door creaked open loudly. She heard a harsh laugh and the sounds of a struggle. "No," she murmured quietly to herself. "No, please no." Hadn't the man already been through enough? Trace was tortured at least every other day. How much more could he take? Why the hell were they doing this to them? And it wasn't just them. At any given time there were normally at least two more prisoners down in the Dungeon with them. The guards seemed to take extreme pleasure in picking their next prey to put on the torture block.

Turning around slowly, Gypsy slid back toward the wall until her backside rested against it, her arms wrapped tightly around her legs, her chin digging into the tops of her knees. Grasping her hands tightly together, she prayed for her friend. He was a good man, a man with a mate at home who needed him. She prayed that she and Trace would both escape their hell soon. Letting her hair fall forward until it covered her eyes, Gypsy peeked through the dirty, tangled mass of dark brown strands to watch what was happening on the other side of her cell.

Two men had managed to drag Trace over to the table where they liked to restrain their prisoners while inflicting pain on them. He fought weakly when they hefted him up on top of the table and hooked the heavy chains that surrounded his body to heavy metal rings bolted into the four corners. Trace did not say a word as the men jeered at him, calling him names and laughing loudly, letting him know what they had planned for him this time. He was so strong and fierce, ignoring their snide comments as he glared at them, his eyes full of hatred. The chains dug into his wrists as he tugged uselessly on them. Her heart ached at the thought of the pain he was about to endure. She knew he would suffer in silence, but inside, he would be screaming.

Struggling to her feet, Gypsy moved to the front of her cell and gripped the bars tightly. She could not just hide on the floor while they tortured Trace. If it wasn't for him, she would have lost the will to live a long time ago. "Stop," *she cried out as one of the men slammed something down on Trace's leg.* "Stop, dammit! Leave him alone, you bastards!"

She stilled, her hands tightening on the bars as one of them turned to leer at her. "Don't worry, sweetheart," *the man sneered darkly,* "Your turn is next." *Gypsy's whole body shook at the threat. It would not be the first time they had come for her, and it certainly wouldn't be the last. Tearing her eyes from his, she returned her gaze to the only friend she had, tears sliding down her cheeks at the sight of the blood and bruises covering his body.*

Trace locked his eyes with her, shaking his head slightly in warning. Grasping the bars tightly, she glared back at him in defiance. When Trace refused to look away, his gaze demanding she back down, Gypsy fought with herself before finally sighing in defeat. Knowing she would only piss him off more if she continued to yell, Gypsy stood and watched in silence as tears streamed down her face. Trace took blow after blow to his abdomen and legs, his body bowing up in pain. Not once did he utter a sound. She knew he would not give the bastards the satisfaction of letting them know how much pain he was in, but she knew. She was in his mind, feeling each blow as if it were her own. She always stayed with him, a subtle presence in his mind, while he was being tortured. He hated it, but there was no way in hell she was going to let him go through that alone, and he wasn't strong enough to push her out.

Gypsy's heart ached as she stood watching her friend, vowing to stay connected with Trace while he went through hell, no matter what. She wanted him to know that he was not alone. When he tried to shove her out of his mind, just like he always did, she fought him, stubbornly refusing to allow him to suffer by himself.

When they decided they were finished, the men removed Trace from the table and shoved him roughly to the floor. Grabbing him by his arms, they dragged him back to his cell, throwing him inside and hooking his chains to the hooks on the wall before slamming the door shut.

Moving quickly back to the far corner of her cell, Gypsy cowered as far away from the men as she could. Sitting down, she pulled her legs up close to her body and rested her forehead on her knees, allowing her dingy hair to hide her face. She prayed the men left her alone this time. So far, all they had done was beat and starve her, but she was afraid one of these days it would escalate into more.

*Gypsy cringed when she heard the key enter the lock on her cell door. Chuckling lowly, one man said, "*It's your turn, bitch. Come here and take your punishment like a good little girl.*"*

*Her whole body shaking, Gypsy raised her head and glared at them. If Trace could be strong, so could she. Slowly standing, her whole body shaking in fear, Gypsy clenched her trembling fingers tightly into fists. "*Fuck you,*" she snarled, her dark brown eyes snapping in anger. "*If you want me, come and get me.*" Staring into the man's evil gaze, Gypsy almost wished she had stayed curled up on the floor, but she was so tired of living in fear. It wasn't going to change the outcome. No matter* *what, these assholes were going to hurt her. However, when one of the guards reached out and grabbed her arm, squeezing it tightly, she could not stop the terrified scream that escaped.*

"Hush, Sweetheart," Gypsy heard a low voice say as she reared up in bed, screams tearing from her throat. Eyes wide in terror, she flinched from the hand that gently stroked her arm, trying to pull away. "Look at me, Gypsy," the deep, male voice commanded quietly. "Look at me. You are safe, Mate. No one is ever going to hurt you again."

Mate? Gypsy thought as she struggled to focus on the man standing beside her. What was a mate? Hell, she didn't know. She didn't know much of anything. She wasn't even sure she remembered her own name. Everyone kept calling her Gypsy, and since they acted like they knew her, she assumed they must be right. Not only that, but it felt right.

Sighing in frustration, she leaned back against the bed, resting her head on the pillow. Skimming her eyes discreetly over the man, Gypsy felt her heart flutter when their eyes met. Who was he? She could drown in his deep, chocolate-colored gaze. Her eyes wandered over his thick, dark hair to his strong jawline, finally coming to rest on his firm, sensual lips. She had seen him before. He'd been in her room several times when she had woken in the middle of the night. Normally he stood by the window, looking out into the darkness.

The first week in the hospital, Gypsy had floated in and out of consciousness, always losing her hold on reality before she could question him. She was so weak and malnourished that her body required an enormous amount of sleep. The last time she had seen him, he was talking quietly with the doctor. Not wanting to interrupt, she tried to stay awake to find out who he was, but ended up falling asleep again, and he was gone the next time she came to. She felt as if she knew him, even though something told her she'd never met him before coming to the compound. That's what they called the place where she was currently staying; the White River Wolves compound.

Glancing out the window, Gypsy frowned as she realized it wasn't dark outside. Normally, the man only came at night as far as she knew, but the way the sun barely peeked through the blinds suggested it was early morning. As much as she wanted to find out who he was, she was suddenly aware of how she must look to him. The swelling on her face had lessened, but several dark bruises remained. The nurses had helped her shower and wash her hair, so at least it wasn't the ratty, dirty mess it had been when she arrived. The blankets hid the dark bruising that covered the majority of her thin, battered body. Lowering her head, she rubbed self-consciously at the cast on her arm, wincing in pain. She wasn't sure why it mattered. She didn't want anyone looking at her twice after the hell she had just endured. Her brow furrowing, she wondered exactly what that was supposed to mean. What hell had she been through? Her mind was one messed up, confusing place lately.

Narrowing her eyes, Gypsy struggled to recall what upset her in the first place. Why did the man feel the need to try and calm her? What had she been screaming about? *A dream*, she thought, her brow furrowing. She'd had a dream. *More like a nightmare*, she thought with a grimace. Images of someone in unbearable pain as he was beaten over and over again with a tire iron flashed through her mind, and then there was nothing. Her head pounding, Gypsy fought to bring the images back, but the harder she fought, the harder it became to concentrate. The nightmare was just lost to her.

Groaning softly, Gypsy tried to get more comfortable in the hospital bed, fighting to push back the pain that flowed through her. Her entire body ached, and no matter which way she turned, there was no relief. Closing her eyes, Gypsy took a deep breath, trying to relax her tense muscles. Feeling the hand still stroking her arm lightly, she allowed herself to take comfort from the stranger's gentle touch. "Who are you?" she asked softly as she struggled to open her eyes again.

Her head pounded as she tried to remember something...anything. Not for the first time, Gypsy wondered if she should know the man with the captivating eyes and deep, sexy voice. For some reason, she felt like she should. Squeezing her eyes tightly shut, she cried out as a bolt of pain shot through the back of her head.

"Nurse!" the man yelled, his hand tightening slightly on her arm. "I need a nurse in here!"

She heard the soft pitter patter of feet as someone quietly entered the room. "What can I do for you, Sir?" a soft, timid voice asked.

"She's in pain," he growled, his voice low and demanding. "Get her something for it, now." Gypsy felt sorry for the nurse, but the man's gruff, commanding tone somehow made her feel safe. She had a feeling she had not felt that way in a very long time.

"Your name?" Gypsy whispered again, moaning as another sharp sliver of pain sliced though her head. For some reason, it was very important she know his name before she lost the fight and succumbed to the darkness that threatened to consume her.

"Slade," she heard him mutter from his position by the side of her bed. "Slade Dawson." She could tell he'd moved away slightly, but he had not left her. As the shooting pain in her head became almost too much to bear, Gypsy softly whispered his name before finally allowing the darkness to overtake her.

3

S lade sat in a chair by the hospital bed watching Gypsy sleep. The nurse had given her something for the pain immediately after she'd lost consciousness. As his eyes traced the pale, bruised features of her beautiful face, Slade growled lowly, his hands clenching and unclenching in anger. His tiny, delicate mate lay in pain and fear, and there wasn't a damn thing he could do about it. The men who hurt her were already dead, killed by RARE when they rescued Gypsy and Trace just days before from a Colombian drug lord. If not, he would hunt them down and take out every last one of them himself.

Fuck, he had never thought he would actually find his fated mate. Not all shifters did. Some searched their whole life for their mates, only to end up living, and dying, alone. Some fell in love and married, even knowing their mates could be out there waiting…like he had.

Leaning forward in the chair, elbows on his knees, Slade bowed his head, sighing deeply. He felt guilt pour through him as he remembered his sweet Sarah. Sarah may not have been his mate, but he had loved her since the day they met. A young lady of seventeen years, she was sweet and innocent. Her long, light blonde hair and bright blue eyes were what attracted him to her at first. Her large heart and gentle nature sealed the deal. Once he had her, he was not able to let her go. Slade married Sarah and loved her for the three years they'd had together.

After Sarah's death, Slade wanted to die himself. Even though they did not share a mate bond, he had been deeply in love with his wife. After losing both her and their baby in childbirth, he lost the will to live. Merely existing, Slade roamed the countryside, drinking and getting into trouble for several years. Looking back, Slade was not proud of some of the things he had done, but at the time, he had a death wish of his own. His wife and child were dead, and he wanted to be, too. Life wasn't worth living without Sarah by his side.

When he finally climbed out of the bottle, Slade decided it was time to get his act together and try to move on. Sarah would not be proud of the man he had become. Hell, he wasn't very happy with himself. She would definitely not have approved of the cage fighting he found himself participating in frequently. It was the only way he could actually feel anything. He was able to block out the emotional pain by substituting it with physical pain. Drunk fighting was not smart, though, and there came a time where he almost didn't walk out of the ring alive. That was what it took to make him realize that even without his Sarah with him, he really was not ready to die. It was a long, hard road, but finally he managed to put it all behind him and move on. A part of him still missed Sarah, but time had dulled the pain and sadness. Now he chose to remember the laughter and good times they had shared instead of the dark despair caused by her death.

Slade raised his head and gazed at the lovely woman still asleep on the bed in front of him. It had been over one hundred years since Sarah passed away. He was a normal, full-blooded male. He had sex when he felt the need to, but it was always rough, and never with anyone from his pack. Slade did not do love and commitment. He stayed far away from anything that could remotely be classified as a commitment. At least, that was how he had chosen to live life in the years following Sarah's death. Now there was Gypsy. He was going to have to find a way to move on and accept his mate in his life. He didn't have a choice. Mates could not be apart for long periods of time. It was virtually impossible. Already, he felt the pull toward her. Would she want him when she realized he had forsaken their mate bond and married Sarah? Could she forgive him?

Shaking his head, Slade realized that even though he might be able to move on and claim his mate, she definitely was not ready for him. If the numerous bruises, stitches, and broken arm were any indication, not to mention the stench of fear that clung to her, Gypsy may not be ready for the mate bond for a long, long time. She was human. She would not understand what it meant to have a mate. There was also her amnesia to take into consideration. Gypsy did not remember anything prior to waking up in the White River Wolves hospital. She had barely been coherent in the past week that she'd been there, spending most of the time asleep.

Rising in frustration, Slade made his way over to the window. Standing with his hands on his hips, he looked out over the light dusting of snow that blanketed the land beyond the hospital grounds. Raising a hand to rub the tense muscles in the back of his neck, Slade thought about his mate. He knew next to nothing about the woman who lay in the bed behind him, besides the fact that she was stunning and made his cock hard as a rock. It didn't matter that it was, in large part, the mate bond that was making him want her the way he did, he still could not get rid of his need to bury himself deep inside her. Unfortunately, it wasn't anything he would be able to act on for some time. Raking a hand tiredly through his hair, Slade squeezed his eyes shut in exhaustion. He would have to have patience, and that wasn't one of his strongest traits.

"How is she?" a soft voice asked from the open doorway.

Stiffening at the intrusion to his thoughts, Slade turned to face the woman. "Same as when you stopped by the last time."

"And how are you doing?" she asked quietly, her dark green eyes wide and inviting. The open expression on her face urged him to talk to her. A part of him wanted to, but he wasn't sure where to start. He'd never been very good at expressing his feelings.

Placing his hands on his hips, Slade turned to look out the window once again. "It is what it is, Jade," he said shortly. "I can't change anything." Closing his eyes, he sighed tiredly. Glancing at the bed to make sure Gypsy was still asleep, he looked back at Jade. "I have no idea how to help her. I can't give her memories back to her. I can't remove the fear that haunts her." Realizing he was voicing his own fears to Jade, he laughed roughly. "It seems you found your calling. You are pretty decent at the counselor gig, aren't you?"

Returning his smile, Jade responded lightly, "I hope I am. I love helping people. It's so much better than what I was doing before."

Wincing, Slade turned back to the window. Jade had been through so much in her young life. When she was just a child, she was captured by a man known only as the General. She was held for several years in a desolate area in an Arizona desert. He didn't know the specifics, but he knew she was rescued by RARE. Angel, the leader of RARE, was Jade's mother, and Jade was now mated to one of the men on Angel's team. Even though she was more than qualified to become a part of RARE, Jade had chosen to work as a counselor of sorts at the hospital, and she seemed to be very good at her job.

Slade had been closed off for so many years, unwilling to share his emotions and feelings with anyone after his wife and child died. Now he had the chance to move on. To move on with a mate that he had forsaken for another woman. A mate who had lost her memory and had no idea what a shifter even was. Slade let a low growl of frustration escape. His life was so fucked up.

Hearing a soft moan, Slade swung around toward the bed. It seemed as if Gypsy was having another nightmare. She'd had several over the past few days. Even though Slade wasn't always there with her, he heard about them from the nurses. Unfortunately, she never seemed to remember them.

"No," Gypsy cried out softly as she thrashed around

wildly. "Sari! Sari! Please, please don't hurt my sister," she begged as tears ran down her face. "Sari!"

Slade stayed where he was when Jade moved to the bed and placed a gentle hand on Gypsy's arm. Murmuring softly to her, Jade leaned in closer and gently stroked a hand down her long, dark hair. As he watched, Gypsy slowly quieted down and slipped back into a deep sleep.

Jade stayed by her side for several moments, before finally stepping back and turning to the door. "Thank you, Jade," Slade said roughly.

Jade smiled, "One touch from you would have done the same thing. A mate's touch is very calming." With one last gentle smile, she left the room, letting the door close softly behind her.

Just as Slade took a step toward Gypsy, the phone in his pocket vibrated. His eyes narrowing, Slade retrieved it to check the caller ID. Seeing Chase's number, he answered quietly. "Yes, Alpha."

On the other line Chase ordered roughly, "I need you in my office now, Slade. Xavier's been shot."

"I'm on my way," Slade responded shortly. After one last look at his mate, Slade quickly left the room. Five minutes later, he was standing in front of Chase's desk listening to a breakdown of what they had figured out so far regarding the shooting, which was basically nothing.

"The son of a bitch had to have been outside the gates of the compound. I couldn't find a trace of an unknown scent anywhere," Chase growled as he rose from his chair and started pacing around the room. Stopping in front of the huge window in his office, he ordered, "I need you to take some of your enforcers and case the area around the outside of the fence. Then spread out until…"

"With all due respect, Alpha," Slade interrupted, praying he didn't get his ass kicked with the mood Chase was in lately, "we would need to go at least a mile out if it was a sniper, even further if we can't find anything."

"Then what in the hell are you waiting for?" Chase growled. "Take your enforcers and go!"

Bowing his head in submission, Slade responded quietly, "Yes, Sir." Without another word, Slade left the alpha's office. Taking out his phone, he sent a text to four of his best enforcers, including Bran, the pack's beta. He was going to need all of the help he could get if he wanted to come up with something before dark.

SIGHING DEEPLY, Chase Montgomery raked a hand through his thick, dark hair. He hated to be such a prick to his head enforcer, but he could not seem to control his temper lately. Grunting in annoyance, he placed a hand against the cool glass of the window. Chase shook his head in disgust as he remembered flying through that same window in his wolf form just a week earlier. He knew he was being stubborn. He could contact RARE and have them there shortly as long as they weren't out of town on a mission. With their abilities, the team could figure out what the hell was going on a lot quicker than Chase and his enforcers could. But, there was a reason he did not want to call RARE in on this, and her name was Angel Johnston.

Not only was Angel the leader of the highly trained mercenary team, she was also Chase's mate; A fact that she did not want to acknowledge, even though she had bitten him months before starting the bonding process herself. Stepping away from the window before the thought of Angel's rejection caused him to shatter it again, Chase turned and left his office. He needed to check on Xavier and Aiden. His sorry excuse for a love life would have to wait.

4

Gypsy snuggled deeper into the warm blankets enveloping her. A soft smile curved her full lips as she envisioned dark hair, deep brown eyes, and a strong jawline. "Slade," she breathed softly, a small shiver running up her spine.

At the sound of her own voice, her eyes sprang open and she cautiously looked around the room. The hospital...she was in the hospital. When she was sure she was alone, Gypsy pushed herself up into a sitting position on the bed, crying out at the pain that raced through her body. Gasping for air, she slowly lowered herself back to the pillow. Closing her eyes tightly, she cringed as she saw a hand coming toward her and yanking her up off of the cold, hard ground by her hair. Another hand smacked her repeatedly across the face, the person yelling something she could not make out. It had to be a part of her memory resurfacing. Gypsy pushed down the fear, and clenched the sheets in her hands tightly as she fought to remember more.

"You bitch," a deep voice growled, his hand tightening around her arm as he shook her roughly. "I bring you what extra food I can hide from my boss. If he found out what I was doing, he would throw me down here with you. As much as I may want to fuck you, I don't want to share a cell with you." *Gypsy sobbed, begging the man to stop when he began to bend her arm in a way it wasn't supposed to bend. "What food I bring down here is a gift for you! Not for the piece of shit in the cell next to yours. I will teach you to give away my gifts." Struggling to catch her breath, she cried out in pain as a sharp crack split through the air and pain shot up through her arm.* Gypsy knew it was just a memory, but it felt as if she were reliving it. Clutching her broken arm, she sat back up and screamed loudly over and over again, trying to push the memories back down.

She flinched when a gentle hand touched her shoulder. "You're okay, Gypsy," a sweet voice said. "It's going to be all right. You aren't back there in that prison cell. You are in a hospital at the White River Wolves compound. You are safe. No one is going to hurt you again." The soft touch and kind voice helped to calm her terror, and Gypsy slowly crumpled back against the bed again, her head resting on the soft pillow.

Turning to the woman she now recognized as Jade, she let the tears flow freely down her face. Shaking in fear and pain, Gypsy whispered, "I don't know if I will ever feel safe again."

Jade lightly brushed a stray strand of hair out of Gypsy's eyes as she replied confidently, "Yes, you will. You aren't alone now, Gypsy. You have Slade, Trace, and me. Hell, you have the whole White River Wolf pack behind you. Slade is their head enforcer. They will do anything for him. I promise you, you never need to be afraid again."

Gypsy frowned in confusion at Jade's choice of words. Exactly what was the White River Wolves compound? And what did Jade mean by the wolf pack protecting her? Maybe they lived in a place for endangered wolves. She had heard of places similar to that...at least she thought she had. There were obviously a lot of questions that needed answers, but right now, she just did not have the energy to ask them all. Looking down in shame, Gypsy told Jade, "I never used to be afraid of anything. I was the strong one. Until they broke me."

"Trust me when I say this, Gypsy Layne," Jade growled, her hand gently squeezing Gypsy's shoulder, "you are far from broken. You are just a little lost right now. You will find your way soon." The promise in Jade's gaze filled Gypsy with hope and belief that she would not stay the empty shell of the person she now felt herself to be. "You are slowly beginning to remember things. Once your memory returns, you will be so much stronger."

Looking up at Jade in surprise, Gypsy murmured, "I am starting to recall some things. I have all of these pictures running through my head sporadically, and it's like I have to fit all of the pieces of a puzzle together. And there is no rhyme or reason as to what I remember. I can't tell you for sure that my name is Gypsy, but I do know my favorite food is pizza. I love the color blue. I enjoy singing, but I can't carry a tune." Shaking her head, Gypsy whispered, "Why can I remember the little, trivial things, but not something like my own name? And Sari? You would think I would remember my own sister." When Jade told her the week before that she had a sister in the hospital with her, one who had suffered as much, if not more than Gypsy at the hands of an evil drug lord, Gypsy had not wanted to believe her. She couldn't remember any family, and the thought of someone else suffering the way she was, broke her heart. She could understand forgetting some things, but family? It had been a couple days before she was able to talk Jade into helping her down the hall to Sari's room. She had wanted to see the girl with her own eyes, hoping that if she saw her sister, it would help her memory return. She did not recognize Sari, but was encouraged by the fact the girl's features were very similar to her own. Sari had long, blonde hair, where Gypsy's was a dark brown in color, and pale skin to Gypsy's more tanned tone. But, even with that, it was obvious they were related.

Gypsy had gone back a couple of times to see Sari, but every time she visited, the girl had been asleep. She had sat by Sari's bed and held her hand, tears flowing freely down her face as she thought about the things she'd been told her sister had gone through at the hands of a madman. Her visits didn't last very long because she was so weak herself, but she went because she didn't want Sari to feel as alone as she did.

Interrupting Gypsy's thoughts, Jade covered her hand and smiled gently. "Doc Josie and I believe you have what is called Dissociative Amnesia. We think it's been caused by the trauma you have been through these past few months. It is common to not only forget the traumatic event itself, but to have huge holes or gaps in your memory."

"Will I ever regain all of my memories?" Although she had no problem with forgetting the torture and horror she had been put through, Gypsy wanted to remember life before her time spent in hell. There were so many questions she had, so many things left unanswered.

"Statistically, it could go either way. Some patients eventually remember everything, while others never recall pieces of their past. Your memories still exist, Gypsy, you've just buried them deep after all that you have been through. If you want my personal opinion, I think you are suppressing them. You don't want to remember because it's too painful."

Gypsy thought about Jade's words for a minute before she admitted softly, "I do remember some things about my captivity. At least, I think that I do." Jade's hands tightened on hers, but she stayed silent. "I have these dreams. Horrible nightmares of pain and suffering. Trace is in them. They are hurting him, beating him, but there's nothing I can do. I try to stop them..."

"They aren't just dreams, Gypsy," Jade said softly, her emerald eyes glistening with unshed tears. "Trace was tortured for months. The chances are very good he would have died without you there to encourage him to push on."

"No." Gypsy shook her head in denial. "He would have lived. For you." Gypsy frowned as she struggled to remember. "He fought to come home to you."

There had been a loud roar, and then the sounds of Trace in the cell next to hers fighting against the chains that bound him. His eyes had seemed to glow and his hands had changed, what looked like claws emerging. "Stop, Trace. You have to stop," Gypsy demanded weakly. "Conserve your strength. You aren't going to get out of those chains. You have tried so many times."

Trace hissed, "I have to, Gypsy. I have to get home to her."

Her eyes full of sympathy, Gypsy whispered, "And you will, my friend. But you have to calm down. You can't let them see you like this. They can't know your secrets."

As the memory faded away, a nurse entered the room, Gypsy's chart in her hands. "I just need to check your vitals," she said, placing the chart on the foot of the bed. "You have been making remarkable progress, Gypsy."

Fucking hurts. I need to get to her. Need to protect her. Gypsy froze as the words seemed to seep into her mind. It felt as if someone was in her head with her. She could feel him there. *Need to take care of her.* Gypsy gasped out loud as she was suddenly consumed with pain, fear, and a strong determination to protect someone, but she had no idea who. *Can't let anyone hurt her. Need help.* Then, he was just gone, like he'd never been there in the first place, taking all of the overwhelming emotions with him.

"We are going to up your daily physical therapy to include small walks around the hospital," the nurse was saying. "We need to get your strength back up, and the small trips you are taking to the bathroom aren't enough."

"O…Okay," Gypsy stammered, trying to focus on what the woman was saying. Had that really happened? It couldn't have. No way was someone inside her head…was he?

"You're trembling, dear," the nurse said as she gently encircled Gypsy's wrist with her hand, placing two fingers over her pulse. "Are you all right?"

Gypsy looked up into kind, light blue eyes and swallowed hard. "Yes. Yes, I'm okay," she lied. What the hell was going on? She had felt that man's pain, and heard the terror in his voice. It was real. It had to be. Was it a memory? She didn't think so. It didn't sound like Trace's voice, and as far as she knew, he was the only one she had really interacted with in the Dungeon.

"Gypsy? What's wrong?" Jade questioned softly. "Talk to me. Let me help you."

Poor child seems scared to death.

Gypsy's eyes widened and she yanked her arm away from the nurse, scrambling off the bed and almost falling to the floor. What the hell was going on? That had been the nurse's voice. She'd heard it loud and clear in her head. Stumbling to the chair in the far corner, Gypsy collapsed onto it, silently screaming inside.

Jade knelt in front of her, but Gypsy shrank back away from the other woman, flinching when Jade placed a hand lightly on her shoulder. Immediately, Gypsy started to calm down, a feeling of peace filling her. *That's it. There's nothing to be afraid of. Rest.*

Unable to fight the subtle push Jade sent her way to force her compliance, Gypsy slowly let her eyes drift closed. *What's happening to me?* Unaware of the surprise in Jade's eyes, Gypsy fell into a deep sleep, leaving all of the fear and confusion behind.

———

GYPSY WAS AWAKENED JUST hours later by a loud, piercing scream that ripped through the air. She was lying curled up in the chair, a blanket draped over her. Slowly sitting up, she ran a hand through her tangled hair as she wondered what was going on. A scream of terror reached her again, and then there was the sound of several footsteps rushing past her door. Gypsy shoved the covers aside, and bracing her hands on the arms of the chair, careful of her broken arm, she stood weakly on shaky legs. One more scream had her slowly shuffling out of her room and down the hall in the direction of the commotion.

"Gypsy," a female voice yelled. "Gypsy, help me! Please, help me!" Moving faster at the terror in the young female voice, Gypsy ignored the pain and weakness she felt. All she knew was someone needed her, and she had to get to them now. She knew that voice. Who was it? She frowned as images of a young girl in a light blue dress with laughing brown eyes filled her mind. It was Sari, she was sure of it. The girl giggled as she held out a hand to Gypsy. Gypsy blinked, and the vision was gone.

Gypsy followed a nurse into Sari's room and stopped just inside the door, gasping at the sight before her. Cowering on the floor in the corner of the room was her sister. Her beautiful blonde hair was matted around her pale, tear-stained face. "Get away from me!" she cried as she pushed at the nurse's hands. "Don't touch me!"

"I'm not going to hurt you," the nurse said softly, as she tried to capture one of Sari's hands with her own. "We need to get you back in bed, Sari. You need your rest."

"Gypsy," Sari moaned plaintively. "I need Gypsy." Her small, frail shoulders shook with her loud sobs. "Please, I need her."

"I'm here," Gypsy said as she slowly made her way across the room. "Sari, I'm right here." Silence filled the room as everyone looked from Sari to Gypsy. The next thing she knew, Sari was off the floor and in her arms.

"Why didn't you come to see me, Gypsy?" Sari cried, clutching tightly to Gypsy's waist. "I've been so scared without you. They said Philip is dead and he can't get to me, but what if he isn't? What if he comes back?"

Philip, Gypsy thought, her eyes narrowing. He was the bastard who had stolen them from their family and placed them in hell. Her head pounded in pain as an image of a man grabbing hold of Sari by her hair and lifting her off the hard, cold floor of Gypsy's cell swam through her mind. Slowly putting her arms around Sari, Gypsy ran a hand down the girl's hair, her heart clenching at the thought of anyone hurting the terrified child. Sari's whole body shook as she clung to Gypsy.

"We need to get Sari back in bed, Gypsy," Jade said softly as she moved to stand beside them. "Can you help us with that? She needs to lie down."

Gypsy nodded as she guided the weeping girl over to her bed. Sari refused to let go of her, so Gypsy crawled up into the bed and Sari slipped in after her, wrapping her arms tightly around Gypsy's waist, once again. Gypsy hid her own pain as she held the girl close. Letting her head fall to Gypsy's chest, Sari cried.

Motioning for the nurses to leave, Jade came forward and sat on a chair beside the bed. They sat in silence for several minutes before Sari's sobs finally stopped, and Gypsy realized she had fallen asleep.

Running a hand gently down the girl's back, Gypsy whispered raggedly, "Why can't I remember, Jade? Why can't I remember my own sister?"

"Your mind is blocking everything out," Jade replied gently. "It's a way of protecting yourself from the horror of everything you've been through. You will remember when you are ready."

"I'm ready now," Gypsy insisted, her dark eyes snapping with anger. "How can I help Sari if I can't remember what happened to make her this way? To make me this way?" she questioned as she motioned to herself. "How can I protect myself or my sister when I have no idea who I am even protecting us from?"

"That's what you have me for," a deep voice said from the doorway. Gypsy's gaze swung quickly to the man standing in front of her. Her mate. She still had no idea what a mate was. Maybe it was like a soul mate. Her breath hitched as she began to drown in his hypnotic stare. "You just worry about getting better and let me worry about any danger that may be out there," Slade said as he leaned against the doorjamb.

"You can't always be here, Slade," Gypsy murmured as she let her gaze slide down his muscular chest covered in a snug black tee-shirt, down lower over his abs to his lean hips…when her sister moaned softly in her sleep, Gypsy shook herself out of the direction her thoughts were taking her as she continued, "I need to know what to do when you aren't around. What happens when we go home?" Hell, did she even have a place to go home to? "I don't even know how to make a fist, let alone how to fight off someone who would want to hurt me."

"Then I will teach you," Slade replied as his gaze wandered over her face. "I will teach you how to protect yourself, but not until Doc Josie approves it."

"I'm so confused," Gypsy admitted quietly, her gazed going from Slade to Jade. "I have so many questions. If only I could remember."

"You are starting to, Gypsy. Give it time. Don't try and push it." She knew Jade was right, but time was something Gypsy didn't feel she had. She shivered as a feeling of trepidation moved through her. Something or someone was coming for her. Somehow, she knew it.

"Xavier is ready for you, Slade," a soft, feminine voice interrupted from the hallway. "The doctor said not to stay long. He is unconscious, so won't be of any help right now, but you can still check on him."

"Xavier?" Gypsy asked, a shiver running up her spine. It was a bad sign, she somehow knew. The name meant something, but she had no idea what.

"One of my enforcers. He was shot today while out on patrol. I need to check on him and talk to the doctor. I'll be by to see you later tonight, Gypsy."

After Slade left, Gypsy leaned back against the pillow, feeling her eyes droop tiredly. "Why don't I help you back to your bed?" Jade's voice drifted over her, but Gypsy didn't respond. She didn't have the energy to move, much less walk down the hall back to her room. Within minutes she was sound asleep, cradling her sister in her arms, Xavier's name running through her mind.

5

The light touch on her shoulder startled her, and Gypsy sat up quickly. Looking around the room, she frowned when she realized she was once again back in her own bed. "Slade thought you might be more comfortable in here," the nurse said quietly. It was a different nurse than the one who had been in her room before. Gypsy thought her name was Maria, but she couldn't remember for sure. They seemed to switch her nurses quite a bit for some reason, and she had never been very good with names. "He brought you back about an hour ago. Don't worry," she rushed to assure Gypsy, "Sari is still sleeping." When Gypsy didn't respond, she went on, "I brought you some dinner. I hope you like roast beef and mashed potatoes with brown gravy." She placed the food on a tray in front of Gypsy, a small smile on her lips.

"Thank you," Gypsy finally said quietly. Absently replying to the nurse's goodbye, Gypsy slowly pushed the tray of food away and climbed out of the bed. Something was not right. She wasn't sure what it was, but she knew she needed to find out. Walking to the door, Gypsy opened it and glanced down the hall. All was quiet, except for the soft murmur of voices at the counter by the doors leading to the lobby area. Turning down the hall in the other direction, Gypsy slowly started walking, unsure of her destination. Passing her sister's room, she glanced in to see that Sari was indeed still asleep, facing away from the doorway.

Continuing on, Gypsy passed three more rooms before she finally found what she was looking for. Opening the door to the very last room at the end of the hallway, she quietly slipped inside. Lying on the bed was a young man, no more than twenty-five or twenty-six years old. A white sheet covered the lower half of his body, while a stark white bandage was wrapped around his chest.

Stopping by the bed, Gypsy reached out and slowly smoothed a lock of light brown hair back from his forehead. He was so still, almost as if he was dead, but she knew he wasn't. It was strange, but she could sense the blood flowing through his veins and the slow thud of his heart beating weakly. This must be the enforcer Slade was talking about earlier. Xavier. Unsure why she was there, of exactly what had drawn her to him, Gypsy moved a chair that was sitting in the corner of the room next to the bed and sat down. Cautiously, she reached out and covered his hand with one of hers, shivering at the coldness she felt. That was definitely not right. She knew the man was alive, she could *feel* it.

Placing her other hand on his arm, Gypsy lowered her head and prayed. Something had guided her to this room, showing her this man needed her help; help she was unsure how to give. Why was she here? What was her purpose?

Gypsy stiffened when the low thump of Xavier's heartbeat began to beat loudly in her ears. She shivered when she felt something stir deep within her; seeming to come alive and send an energy flowing through her. Her brow furrowed as her vision began to waiver, and she moaned softly as tremors coursed through her body. Gypsy moaned, clutching Xavier's hand desperately as pain slammed into her, and she felt utter terror. She knew she was dying and wasn't ready to go. She had so much to live for. Someone was out there who needed her. She had to protect her above all else.

Gasping, Gypsy tried to catch her breath as she suddenly realized what was happening. She had done this before. She *knew* she had. She wasn't the one in so much pain that it felt like her chest was on fire. It was Xavier. He was hurting, suffering horribly, terrified he would never wake up again. He could feel himself slowly leaving this world, and he refused to go without a fight. This was why she was here. She needed to help him. She had to bring him back to the land of the living. Taking several deep breaths, Gypsy closed her eyes and tried to remember what to do. She refused to let him die, not when she *knew* she could save him. Before she knew what was happening, she found herself somehow merging and connecting fully with the enforcer. It was almost as if they were one.

Xavier felt like he was drowning, the pain almost too much to bear. There was fear and confusion, and he felt so alone. He didn't fully understand what was happening to him. He wanted to just drift away, to let all of the misery and agony go, but somehow he knew if he did, he might never see the people he cared about again. And there was one woman he needed to be with. One he loved with all of his heart, even though she had no idea; his mate.

Xavier, Gypsy said, her voice a soft whisper in his mind, *listen to me. It is time to come back now. You are needed here.* When there was no response, Gypsy started to worry. It was like he had not heard her at all. He should have heard her. She knew she was doing this right. She remembered, dammit. She knew how to save him. He just needed to hear her voice. If he listened, she could connect with him and guide him back to the living. *Xavier, you will come back now,* she demanded. *Your mate needs you. You must come back to protect her.*

At first there was no response, then she heard, *Mate.* His voice was faint, almost nonexistent, but he had responded. That was what mattered.

Suddenly, there was the sound of a loud, blaring noise in the background followed by several voices, but Gypsy ignored them. *Yes, your mate. She needs you. Mates can't live without one another, Xavier. You know that. She is the other half of your soul. You need each other.* It would seem she remembered what a mate was now, too. *You can't leave her alone.*

Sweat beaded up on Gypsy's forehead and her body began to tremble uncontrollably. It was a fight to stay connected with the enforcer, but she refused to let go, because if she did, she knew he would be lost forever.

"Get her the hell away from him," Gypsy heard Doc Josie order. "Nurse, get me the paddles!"

"No!" Jade yelled forcefully. "Do not move her!"

"Jade, he is going to die," the doctor argued fervently. "I have to get near Xavier to save him, and I can't do that with Gypsy holding onto him."

"You can't save him now, Josie," Jade replied woodenly. "Only Gypsy can. And if you tear them apart, you may lose them both."

It was true. What Gypsy was doing was extremely dangerous. She was now deep inside Xavier's mind. If something happened to him, if he died, she could very well die with him. Blocking out the sound of the doctor swearing and the sudden sound of Chase Montgomery's voice demanding to know what the hell was going on, Gypsy concentrated solely on Xavier.

Tell me about your mate, Xavier, she whispered. *Tell me what she's like. What's her favorite color? What does she like to do?* She had to get him talking so she could deepen their connection.

There was silence and then *Beautiful...she's beautiful.* It was hard for him to get the words out, but he did. Resisting the urge to push him for more, Gypsy waited. *Must protect her. In danger.*

Do you think whoever shot you will go after your mate? Gypsy asked. If that was the case, they would need to keep a close eye on her.

Always in danger, Xavier rasped. *The General wants her back.*

Gypsy had no idea who the General was, but she could feel Xavier fighting. The pain was engulfing him, but the thought of his mate was making him push on. *Then you need to come back with me so you can help us protect her, Xavier. I know it's hard, but you can do this. For her.*

Tell my brother he must keep her safe. Xavier breathed.

Tell Aiden to watch over her for me.

Get your ass back here and tell him yourself, Gypsy growled. Screw this, she had never been known for her patience, and she refused to sit back and let Xavier give up. *I'm going to give you a little kick start, and then you need to fight like hell. You hear me, Xavier? You fight! Your mate needs you!* Moving one of her hands to his chest, Gypsy placed it over his heart, ignoring a deep growl that filled the room. Squeezing her eyes shut tightly, she concentrated on the flow of energy running throughout Xavier's body. Right now, it was weak and unstable. She needed to give it a little boost; kind of like what the doctor was going to do with the defibrillator, but using some of her own energy instead. It would be much more effective.

Gypsy felt the magic rising in her, collecting in her body and rolling around until it grew into one large mass. Sparks flew from her fingertips when she kicked it out of herself and into Xavier, crying out at the jolt of lightening that raced through her and then into him. There was a collective gasp of shock in the room, and then complete silence except for a long, loud beep that sounded from the monitor beside the bed, before it began to beat in a steady rhythm.

Gypsy moaned as she collapsed onto Xavier's chest, too weak to move. "Gypsy!" she heard Slade yell. He was there. Her mate was there. Oh shit, Slade was her mate. She knew exactly what that meant now.

As Slade leaned down and gathered her up into his arms, Gypsy struggled to get out what she needed to say before she passed out. "Aiden," she gasped. "Xavier needs him."

"What the hell is she talking about?" a voice roared.

"What did she do to my brother?"

Her eyes fluttering open, Gypsy gazed into a face that matched the one in the bed next to her. They were almost identical twins. Letting her head fall weakly against Slade's shoulder, she whispered, "Xavier wants you to watch over his mate. He said she is in danger."

"Xavier doesn't have a fucking mate," Aiden growled, his dark eyes glittering in anger.

Gypsy's brow furrowed in confusion. "He does. He told me."

"I think I would know if my brother had a mate," Aiden sneered, pushing past her to stand near Xavier. Slade growled in warning, pulling Gypsy closer to him. "What the hell did you do to Xavier?"

"She saved his life," Jade said calmly, stepping forward to stand near Gypsy. "If she hadn't done what she just did, your brother would be dead now."

"I think he's going to make it," Doc Josie said in awe from where she stood on the other side of Xavier's bed checking his vitals. "Whatever Gypsy did, it's working."

Clutching tightly to Slade's shirt, Gypsy insisted, "Aiden, you must listen to me." When the man turned her way, she went on before he could respond, "Your brother said someone called the General is after her. That he wants her back." At the collective gasp in the room, she said, "I don't know who that is. Do you?"

Aiden's eyes narrowed dangerously. "Slade," he growled lowly, "Is she messing with me?"

"Gypsy would have no idea who the General is," Slade snarled. "She's been locked in a fucking cell in the basement of a drug lord and tortured for months. She was rescued just over a week ago." When Aiden's eyes widened in horror, Slade finished, "And if you ever disrespect my mate like that again, pup, I will tear your fucking throat out."

"Gypsy," the calm voice of the alpha floated throughout the room, a slight push of power following it. Slade backed away slightly from Aiden, his threat still hanging in the air, before turning to face Chase. "Did Xavier tell you who she is? Several women were rescued from a number of different facilities the General had last year, and many of them live with us now. None of us were aware that one of them is his mate."

Shaking her head, Gypsy whispered, "No, I'm sorry. He never said her name." Pain sliced through her head, and she fought to remain conscious as she continued softly, "I saw her in his mind, though. Blonde hair. Beautiful."

"Show me," Jade said, placing a hand gently on Gypsy's arm.

Unsure exactly what to do, Gypsy brought up an image in her mind of the woman Xavier was thinking of, before she finally allowed herself to slump against Slade in exhaustion.

"Janie," Jade whispered in shock.

A loud roar filled Gypsy's ears, and she whimpered in agony, her body beginning to shake uncontrollably. "Slade." His name was torn from her, a plea for help. Without another word, Slade walked past his alpha and through the door, quickly taking Gypsy back to her room. She sighed when he placed her down on the cool sheets, closing her eyes and snuggling deep into the covers. Her fatigue was outweighing her pain, and she was out within seconds.

6

G ypsy slept steadily through the night, waking up to the early morning light streaming in through the blinds on the window the next day. Bringing Xavier back from the dead had taken a lot out of her and it was a struggle to keep her eyes open. She almost allowed herself to fall back asleep, but she wanted to check on her sister and the enforcer.

After several failed attempts, Gypsy was finally out of bed and making her way to the bathroom when there was a light knock on the door. One of the nurses entered the room, smiling widely when she saw Gypsy on her feet. "Good morning! We've been waiting for you to wake up. How are you feeling?"

Resting a hand on the doorframe to the bathroom, Gypsy returned the nurse's smile with a small one of her own. "Like I've been run over by a semi," she responded with a short, humorless laugh. "I'm sorry, what is your name?" She really needed to make more of an effort to get to know the people in this small community, especially if she was going to be here for a while. Her eyes narrowed as she realized the White River Wolves compound may become her home permanently. If she really was Slade's mate, their destinies were intertwined.

"My name is Becca," the other woman replied with a sweet, gentle smile. "And I'm not really a nurse. I'm actually a scientist. I just help out here sometimes when they need me. From what I've been told, this is the first time in a long time that we have had this many patients staying here at once. You have all definitely kept the nurses on their toes."

Gypsy felt her heart skip a beat at the mention of scientists. A memory from years ago came to her, and she swayed slightly on her feet. They had gone out to dinner, which was a rare treat since money was always so tight. While her mother was ordering their food, Gypsy had accidentally slipped into their waitress's mind and learned the woman feared death was near for her. She had been to the doctor just the day before to have a biopsy done on a lump she had found in her breast, and was waiting to hear back on the results. Gypsy had touched the waitress lightly with her small hand and closed her eyes, concentrating on the one thing she knew when it came for someone...death. After a few moments of silence, she opened her eyes and smiled softly, telling the terrified lady that she had nothing to worry about, death was not coming for her. At the waitress's stunned gaze, her mother stood quickly, grabbing Gypsy's arm and swiftly leaving the restaurant. *Now we have to move again, Gypsy. You know you aren't supposed to use your gifts in public. No one can ever find out about them. The government will want to take you away from me. They will have their scientists run test after test on you to try and figure out why you can do what you do. Your father said it happened to his brother. And if the government doesn't find us, the witch hunters will track you down and try to kill you like they did your father. I have no idea if anyone saw what you did today, so we have to leave, now!* She and her mother had run for years, danger always lurking just around the corner. At least, that was what her mother thought after her father's death. They never actually encountered anyone who was a threat to them until Philip Perez came into their lives.

"Are you okay?" Becca asked, rushing forward to slide an arm around her waist. "Let's get you back to bed."

"No," Gypsy protested, pulling out of Becca's grasp and stumbling into the bathroom. "No, I'm all right. I just need to take a shower."

"Are you sure?"

"Yes," Gypsy insisted, as she turned back to face the other woman. "Thank you for looking in on me. I'm fine, though. I'm going to take a quick shower, and then I would like to check on Sari and Xavier." She knew the irrational fear she was suddenly feeling was not Becca's fault. It was something her mother had instilled in her since she was a small child. When Becca turned away in confusion, opening the door to leave, Gypsy called out, "Becca, wait." Becca turned back, her large eyes full of uncertainty. Unsure what to say after the embarrassing way she had just acted, Gypsy took a deep breath, "It was nice to meet you."

Becca nodded, "You too," was her quick response before she left the room.

Nice way to start off making friends, Gypsy thought,

angry with herself for the way she had overreacted. Becca was a scientist, it was her profession. That did not make her a bad person. It also did not mean she would harm Gypsy if she found out the things she could do. Making a promise to herself to seek out Becca in the future and attempt to form a friendship, Gypsy turned on the shower. Removing the hospital gown she wore, she stepped in, reveling in the hot water that cascaded over her exhausted, sluggish body. She would shower, eat breakfast, and then look in on Sari and Xavier. By then she should feel much more alive and ready to face whatever was thrown at her next.

An hour later, Gypsy made her way down the long hallway to peek in on Sari. It was getting easier to move around, and soon she was standing beside her sister's bed watching the young girl sleep. She looked like an angel, with her long blonde hair splayed out over the pillow, and her face void of pain and fear. It had been so long since Sari had slept peacefully. Reluctant to wake her, Gypsy decided to check on Xavier and let Sari sleep.

Slowly, she made her way down the hallway to the room at the end. Opening the door, she was surprised to see Xavier sitting up in bed. His face was still ghostly pale, and she could feel waves of exhaustion rolling off of him, but he was alive. His eyes slowly opened, and his dark brown gaze rested on her. Holding out his hand, he whispered, "I know you."

Tears filled her eyes as she quickly crossed the room, grasping his hand tightly in hers. "Yes," she responded, a slight catch in her voice. "Yes, you know me."

Xavier's gaze wandered down to their clasped hands,

and then back up to meet hers. "You saved my life," he said in awe. "I was dying. I thought it was my time, but you wouldn't let me go."

Shaking her head, Gypsy brushed a wayward lock of dark hair from his brow. "It wasn't your time to go, Xavier. You have too much left to do on this earth. The great spirit wasn't ready for you."

"How do you know?" he asked, the hand holding hers trembling slightly. "What if he was and we cheated death? What if he comes back for me?"

"He wasn't," Gypsy assured him, smiling gently. "If he was, he wouldn't have let me have you." Xavier nodded, and then leaned his head back against the pillow, squeezing her hand tightly. They sat like that for several minutes before Gypsy finally ventured the question she had wanted to ask since the day before. "Why are you hiding from your mate, Xavier? Why don't you tell her who you are? She must be human, or she would already know."

Xavier opened hooded eyes, glancing toward the door and then back to her. Shrugging, he responded gruffly, "She's been through a lot, and just isn't ready."

It was a vague answer that just raised more questions for her, but Gypsy decided not to ask them. She respected the enforcer's privacy. If he wanted to keep his true identity from Janie, she would not interfere. Rising, she smiled down at him and gently tugged her hand from his. "I need to get back to my sister. I just wanted to make sure you were okay."

"Thank you," Xavier rasped, closing his eyes again. "If you ever need anything, I am forever in your debt."

Reaching out, Gypsy softly trailed her hand over his long, brown hair. "There is no debt to repay, young wolf, but there is a mate you need to claim. Don't wait too long."

Turning to leave, Gypsy stopped short at the sight of Chase Montgomery standing just inside the doorway. How long had he been there? The alpha waited for her to leave the room before following. "What Xavier said in there goes for me, too, Gypsy. If you ever need anything, anything at all, you come to me." He left before she could respond, making his way silently down the hall and out the front door.

———

LATE THAT NIGHT, Gypsy slid out of bed, pulling the blanket off of it and wrapping it snuggly around her shoulders. After sliding on a pair of slippers Jade had given her, she shuffled to the closed door of her room. She refused to stay cooped up in the hospital any longer. She needed to get outside and see the moonlight, to feel the wind in her hair. Gypsy loved the outdoors, especially at night, but she had not been allowed outside once since she had been taken by Philip Perez. When she was rescued and put in the hospital, she had been too weak to try and venture out. Now she felt like she was slowly suffocating, and she couldn't stand it any longer.

Pushing the door open, she glanced up and down the empty hallway before quietly slipping out of the room and slowly, but steadily, making her way toward the front of the hospital. It was after midnight, so the place was empty, except for a handful of staff on duty. No one was sitting at the front counter when she walked past, going through the entranceway, and out the front doors of the building. Hugging the blanket tightly around her body, Gypsy stood at the top of the stairs and took a deep breath, a slow smile spreading across her lips. Tears glistened in her eyes as she started down the stairs that led to a lighted garden area below. She would bet the place was beautiful when the flowers bloomed in season, but right now there was a layer of snow across the ground. Gypsy would not have cared if there had been three feet of snow. She was finally outside, and that was all that mattered to her.

There was a bench in the middle of the garden area, and Gypsy made her way to it, taking a seat on the freezing metal frame. Raising her head to the night sky, she closed her eyes, reveling in the feel of the small breeze sending wisps of hair floating across her face. Cold, brisk air caressed her cheeks, and the light from the moon bathed her face. Her body trembled as the frigid air seeped deep into her bones, but she welcomed it. She never felt as at peace anywhere else as she did outside, in the dark of the night, under the moon. She really needed that calmness and serenity tonight, because ever since she had awoken that morning, memory after memory were coming back, and those memories felt like they were crushing her.

Gypsy took a deep breath, drawing on the energy of the moon, feeling its power surround her, enveloping her. She had always been in tune with the night. Her mother said it was the magic in her blood, calling to her. Her father had been the same way, sitting outside for hours when the moon was full.

Forgetting where she was and who might be watching, Gypsy stood and let the blanket fall to the bench. Holding her arms up high toward the moon, she chanted softly,

Fill me with your power,
Bathe me in your light and energy,
Help heal me, make me stronger.
I accept you for all eternity.

When she turned sixteen, her mother gave her a book that had belonged to her father. It contained information regarding her heritage, told her about some of the powers she would receive, and explained how to harness those gifts. Gypsy had studied the book daily, soaking in information about her father's craft. She had always had a knack for entering minds and extracting information, as well as communicating telepathically with others. She was sometimes able to move things with her mind, but it took a lot of concentration and it caused migraines afterwards, so she chose not to experiment with that gift very often. Another thing she excelled at was bringing people back from the brink of death. She had only used that particular gift four times before Xavier, but it worked on all but one child. To this day, it broke her heart that she had been unable to save the little boy.

One thing she had never been able to do, though, was harm someone. However, she would have killed in a heartbeat when she was in that prison called The Dungeon if she would have had the strength. Unfortunately, they kept her weak and vulnerable, and there was nothing she could do to save herself, her sister, or her friend.

Gypsy hummed quietly as she felt the moon's energy flowing through her, claiming her, and giving her strength. She had missed this so much. She belonged to the night, to the moon and the stars, and they to her.

7

Slade had been awake for forty-eight hours straight. Not only that, but he was already running on little sleep since Gypsy had been brought to the compound, and he was exhausted both mentally and physically. He was no closer to finding the bastard who shot Xavier than he had been the day before, but he wasn't going to be of any use to anyone right now. His head was pounding and he could not concentrate on the smallest task. His mind kept wandering to a certain dark-haired beauty and the miracle she'd performed just hours ago. He would never have believed it if he hadn't seen it with his own eyes, but there was no doubt in his mind that she was the reason Xavier was alive today.

Rubbing his face tiredly, he sighed deeply. He needed to go home to get some rest, but first he wanted to check on his mate. When he left her early this morning, she was sleeping peacefully. He did not want to leave, but it was his duty to find Xavier's shooter and bring him to justice.

He could not do that sitting in the hospital watching Gypsy sleep.

Slade's head was bowed as he walked toward the hospital steps, his hands shoved in the front pockets of his jeans. Just as he placed a foot on the first step, he noticed a slight glow out of the corner of his eye. Glancing in the direction of the garden area, he froze. What the hell?

There, in the middle of the garden, stood Gypsy. Her head was flung back, her arms wide open and reaching toward the stars and moon above. Her eyes were closed, her lips slightly parted. She was wearing nothing except for a hospital nightgown, and he could clearly see the outline of her hardened nipples through the thin material. He felt a sudden tightness in his groin as his cock hardened instantly.

For a moment, his wolf took over and all he could think was that his mate was standing just feet from him, in nothing but her nightgown, and he wanted to feel her against him. He wanted to claim her now, body and soul, for himself. The only thing that stopped him was the bright yellow glow surrounding her. It confused his wolf, and Slade was able to gain control of himself again just in time.

Removing his hands from his pockets, he rearranged his aching cock, groaning lowly. As he watched, Gypsy turned fully in his direction, her dark brown eyes glowing brightly. She was so fucking beautiful, and he was hard as a rock. When her eyes drifted down his body, Slade realized he still held his cock in his hand through his jeans. Unable to stop himself, he stroked the length of it once, then twice. He had no idea what was going on. He knew the mate pull was strong, but this was all together something different. He had been around Gypsy several times in the past week and a half, and while the urge to claim her was hard to ignore, it was nothing like what he was feeling at this moment.

Gypsy lowered her arms and took a step in his direction, the tip of her tongue sneaking out to wet her lips as she whimpered softly. She took another step, reaching an arm out to him. Oh hell, it was obvious she wanted him, too. How was he going to resist?

When she moaned his name on a whispered plea, Slade could not hold still any longer. He crossed the distance between them in an instant, covering her trembling lips with his own. Slipping his hand in her long tresses, he held her still as he outlined her mouth with his tongue, before pushing past her lips to find the sweetness within.

Gypsy returned his kiss, tangling her tongue with his and grasping his hips tightly to pull his hard cock into her soft belly. Sliding his arm around her, he pulled her flush against him, wishing they weren't separated by their clothes. The feel of her breasts against his chest tore another groan from deep within him, but then Gypsy slid her hand inside his coat and under his shirt. The touch of her ice-cold fingers against his skin penetrated through his lust-filled haze, and he stiffened as he pulled back, struggling to get a hold of his emotions. "Gypsy," he rasped as he held her from him. "What the hell is going on? What's happening to us?"

Moaning, she tried to fight Slade's hold to get closer to him again, but he held her still. He wanted nothing more than to take her right then and there, but it just did not feel right. Something was off. "Gypsy," he ground out forcefully, "look at me!"

Gypsy froze, going still in his arms as she slowly raised her gaze to his. Her eyes glowed bright and her body shook, with need or the cold, he wasn't sure. Her small hands clenched tightly into fists and she suddenly fought to get free of him. "Let me go," she whispered, "please, you have to let me go."

Refusing to release her, Slade demanded, "Tell me what this is, Gypsy. Talk to me!"

"The moon," she finally admitted as she stopped struggling and hung her head in shame. Her shoulders slumped and her body shuddered. "It makes me feel things. It makes me…"

Slipping a finger under her chin, Slade tilted Gypsy's head up until her eyes met his. "It makes you more sexual?" he guessed, a shudder running through him.

Gypsy nodded, closing her eyes and refusing to meet his gaze. "Yes. And anyone near me, it would seem."

"Have you done something like that with anyone before?" he demanded. "Have you had sex out under the stars and moon with someone else?" He had no idea why he was asking her something like that. Even though she was his mate, they had just met. He had no control over what she had done or who she had slept with before now. Hell, if he was honest with himself, he had no control over any of it now. Just because they were mates did not mean she had to accept him. She wasn't a shifter. She would not feel the pull as strongly as he did. Gypsy could choose to leave him at any time and there was not a damn thing he could do about it. At that thought, a low growl slipped past Slade's lips and he felt his fangs punch through his gums. He wanted to claim her now. He did not want her to have the chance to leave. If he sunk his teeth deep into her shoulder, she would start feeling exactly what Slade was feeling, and then she would not want to leave.

Before he knew what he was doing, Slade had pulled aside Gypsy's gown and clamped his teeth on her shoulder. He stopped just before he broke the skin, and stood there breathing heavily, fighting himself to pull back. What was he doing? He could not force that kind of decision on her. She would never forgive him. But, as hard as he tried to make himself let her go, he couldn't. She was his, dammit. His. She could not leave him.

"Slade?" Jade's voice floated across the garden. "Slade, you don't want to do that." When he growled lowly but did not move, Jade went on, "Slade, your mate is cold. She is shivering. We need to get her back inside where she will be warm and safe."

His eyes narrowed as Jade's words sank in. Safe. Gypsy was not safe out in the open like this. He had to protect his mate. It was his job to ensure her safety. Pulling back slightly, he gently kissed Gypsy's shoulder, and then nuzzled her neck with his cheek. Through it all, Gypsy stayed absolutely still. "We need to get you back to your room," he whispered, slipping his arm beneath her knees and lifting her up. Cradling her against his chest, he stalked toward the hospital and up the front steps. The doors opened and he walked through, swiftly taking Gypsy down the hall to her room. Laying her on the bed, he stepped back as Jade rushed in with some warm blankets. She quickly wrapped them around Gypsy's shivering body, before sitting beside her, enclosing one of Gypsy's hands in hers.

Slade watched as Gypsy's eyes drifted shut. "Gypsy," he said, shoving his hands into his front pockets, "I'm sorry. I shouldn't have done that."

Gypsy turned away from him, facing the far wall. Slade swallowed hard as he met Jade's concerned gaze, before turning to leave. He had royally fucked that up, and he had no idea what to say or do to fix it.

———

THAT SON of a bitch thought he could touch his woman and get away with it? Nobody touched what belonged to him! Nobody! Slade Dawson would die for that alone. Yes, he knew who the man was. He had done his homework. He knew who they all were; the alpha, the beta, the head enforcer. He even knew who worked in the fucking hospital, every last one of them. It had taken him days to track down all of the information he needed to come up with a plan to infiltrate the White River Wolves compound, but he had it now. He had even managed to find out the wolf's name he almost killed. Almost... somehow the little prick had survived. He didn't know how, but the next time he pulled the trigger, he would make sure the person, or animal, on the other end was dead. A head shot was best. No one would come back from that.

As he watched, the head enforcer exited the front doors of the hospital and made his way to the apartment buildings on the edge of the small town. He supposed it was like a town, with the large business building, apartments, and hospital. He knew a lot of the people worked in the city, commuting daily, but some worked out of that large building. He knew the alpha had a small, but very profitable business. However, no matter how hard he tried, he could not figure out exactly what it was that Chase Montgomery did. That was the one thing at which he had failed to garner information on, and it pissed him off. Not that he really gave a shit, but it could be crucial to his extraction mission.

He waited for Slade to enter the apartment building before he started packing up his gear. Soon, he promised himself, soon his Gypsy would be with him again.

8

Slade grunted as a fist glanced off his jaw and was immediately followed by an uppercut in the ribs. Shit, that hurt. He was distracted and was getting his ass handed to him by a pup. Snarling, Slade jumped back out of the way of the next fist that flew toward his face. Zane laughed, dancing lightly on his heels in a circle around Slade. "Is that all you got, ole man?" he joked with a cocky grin. "I thought you were supposed to be the one training us, not the other…"

Before Zane could finish his sentence, Slade kicked out quickly, connecting with Zane's lower left leg. One powerful punch from Slade's right fist was all it took, and the enforcer was sprawled out on the ground staring up at the sky. Groaning loudly, he complained, "What the hell? Give a man a little warning next time."

"You think your enemies are going to give you any warning?" Slade demanded roughly. "No, they will kill first, not bothering to ask questions later." Stepping back and shaking out his hands, Slade ordered, "Now get off your ass and fight."

Zane looked at him in confusion, but slowly got to his feet. Slade knew he was being unreasonable. He never yelled at his enforcers. They were all good people who took an oath to protect the pack and worked hard to keep their fellow packmates safe. But he was angry and frustrated, both emotionally and sexually. He needed to let out his aggression somehow, and right now, sparring with one of his enforcers was the only way to do it. After fifteen more minutes of beating the shit out of the young wolf, Slade stepped back, breathing heavily. Walking over to his duffle bag, he grabbed a towel to wipe the sweat out of his eyes before motioning to Sable, "You and Sable spar now. Let me see what you can do."

Grabbing a bottle of water, Slade leaned up against the wall to watch the show. It didn't take long for the enforcers to get down to business. They were training in the gym at the White River Wolves compound. Slade required his enforcers to work out and spar with each other at least four days a week. With everything that had happened in the past few months, he wanted them ready for anything. He was still pissed at the way they had allowed the alpha's niece to be taken. He refused to let something like that happen again on his watch.

Slade grunted in approval when Sable inserted a foot between Zane's legs and pushed hard on his shoulders, sending him sprawling onto the ground. Unfortunately, she didn't move quickly enough afterwards and Zane was able to grab her ankles, sweeping her off her feet and knocking her on her ass. Sable was instantly back on her feet and retaliating with a quick jab to Zane's chest, and a roundhouse kick to his gut. Zane may have strength on his side, but Sable was faster, and before long she had the enforcer back on the ground again.

Taking a long drink of his water, Slade let his thoughts stray to Gypsy. It had been two days since he had seen her last. He'd been busy with work. Trying to track down who had shot Xavier was taking up a lot of his time, but if he was honest with himself, he was avoiding his woman.

Shaking his head, Slade crumpled the now empty bottle of water and walked over to the trashcan in the corner to throw it away. His woman. He never thought he would ever have those words associated with himself again. After Sarah died, he figured he would live the rest of his life alone, but now there was Gypsy. Strong, beautiful, magical Gypsy. The mate bond was working fast, and he was already starting to feel things toward her besides lust and desire. Yes, he wanted to slide deep inside her, but he also wanted other things he never thought he would want again. He wanted to hold her close, dry her tears when she cried, be a part of the joy she felt when she laughed. He wanted to share bits and pieces of himself with her, and listen while she talked about her life. He wanted to know what it was like to love again, but he was afraid to let himself find out. He didn't want to fall in love, just to have Gypsy stolen from him like Sarah and his baby had been. He knew he would not survive it this time.

Hearing a loud crack, Slade swung around, looking to where his enforcers were battling it out on the mat. Sable had Zane face down on the ground, her knee pressed into the center of his back. His arm was twisted at an odd angle behind him, and he was screaming in pain, but Sable was not letting up. "You ever make the mistake of touching me like that again, and I will break more than your fucking arm," she growled.

Sauntering over to them, Slade squatted down by Zane. His face was dark red, his lips peeled back revealing his fangs. "Looks like you may have bitten off a bit more than you can chew this time, Zane."

Zane cursed as he struggled to break Sable's hold on him, but no matter how much he moved and bucked, she refused to let him go. "It was an accident, Sable. Get the fuck off me! That hurts!"

"An accident?" Sable snarled, leaning in close to look in his face. "You reached around and grabbed both of my tits in your hands. Not only did you grab them, you squeezed them. Copping a feel like that was no accident." Finally releasing the other enforcer, Sable stood and glared down at him, "I hope you liked it, because not only did it cause you a broken arm, but it cost you my trust and friendship."

"Dammit," Zane spat as he sat up, cradling his arm. "Sable…" but she was already gone.

"So," Slade asked, raising his eyebrows, "was it worth it?"

Zane gulped as he brought his eyes slowly back to Slade. "I'm in trouble, aren't I?"

"Yep," Slade agreed, standing to his full height, glaring down at the young wolf. "Get your ass up, Loctner."

"Where are we going?" Zane stammered, rising first to his knees, then struggling to his feet while still clutching his useless arm. "I need to get this fixed, man. It fucking hurts."

"Oh, you'll get it fixed," Slade agreed, grabbing the kid's uninjured arm and propelling him roughly toward the door. "And then you are going in solitude until the alpha is ready for you."

"The alpha?" Zane squeaked. "But, all I did was touch her boobs. Why do we have to bring the alpha into this?"

"You either get him or me, pup, and trust me, you don't want to mess with me today." Not that talking to Chase was going to be a picnic either. Behavior like that was not tolerated in the pack. You did not touch another pack member unless it was consensual. Zane was going to be in a lot of trouble. It might even cost him his chance at becoming a full-fledged enforcer since he was only a few months into his training. Slade would hate to have to sideline him. He was good at his job, but did not appear to be mature enough to handle it yet.

Walking out of the building, Slade squinted as he waited for his eyes to become accustomed to the bright glare of the sun. It was early in the day, and the way the light shone off the ice-packed snow nearly blinded him. Shit, he'd forgotten his sunglasses. Deciding he better run back and grab them and his coat so he could do a full sweep of the perimeter after dropping Zane off to the cell where he would wait for the alpha, Slade turned to run back in the building. "I have to..." suddenly, he heard a loud noise in the distance and a bullet imbedded itself in the wall just to the right of Zane's head. What the fuck?

Slade grabbed the stunned enforcer and forced him through the doors in front of him. "Get down," he yelled, shoving the pup to the floor and army crawling to where his coat lay in the corner.

Quickly finding his cell phone in the inside pocket, he dialed his alpha. Chase picked up on the first ring. "What the hell is going on?" he demanded loudly.

"Sound the alarm!" Slade growled, quickly slipping off his shoes and sliding out of his jogging pants. "Everyone needs to stay inside! We have a fucking sniper out there, Chase."

Immediately, sirens could be heard throughout the compound. Slade ripped his shirt off over his head as he growled, "The bastard is in the abandoned buildings across the street somewhere. I'm not sure which one. I'm going to shift and go hunting." Slade disconnected the call, not waiting for a response. Tossing the phone to a stunned Zane, he ordered, "Contact the other enforcers and tell them to make sure everyone stays inside. Do not move from this building, Zane. Do you understand me?"

When Zane nodded and started to dial the phone, Slade dropped to all fours and called to his wolf. Within moments a large, dark grey, powerful beast stood where he had just been. Resisting the urge to throw back his head and howl a challenge to whoever had tried to take his head off, Slade ran across the gym and slipped out a door in the back made specifically for the pack in their wolf form.

Sticking to the side of the building, Slade used whatever cover he could find, making his way to the front gate. One of his enforcers opened it from where they were hidden in the guard shack, and he slipped through it quickly. Now he would be on his own crossing the road to the abandoned buildings on the other side. There was no coverage, and he would be an open target. *He's gone.* Slade stopped in his tracks when he heard Gypsy's voice whisper in his mind. *He left right after the sirens went off. He's angry because you moved and he missed you.*

Gypsy? Was it really her? Was she really communicating with him, or was he just imagining it? He hadn't seen her since he left her in her hospital room two nights ago. Jade told him Gypsy needed time and space to think things through, so he had left her alone, even though it had been torture to stay away.

He wants to kill you, Slade. He wants to kill you because of me. His wolf growled at the fear in her voice. Whoever wanted him dead had put it there, and he would pay.

Why? Moving swiftly forward, Slade crossed the road to the buildings beyond. They had been on the land years ago when the pack bought it, and they used them for training rookie enforcers now. Slipping inside one of them, he stopped and raised his head, breathing in deeply, hoping to catch his enemies scent.

He thinks I'm his, and you stole me from him. He wants me back.

Slade paused. *Who is he, Gypsy?*

I don't know, she whispered raggedly. *Why can't I remember, Slade? I remember everything else. I should know who he is. I know I should.*

Slade moved quickly through the building, clearing each room as he went. Gypsy stayed a presence in the back of his mind throughout his search. He could feel her there, lending him her strength and support, as he moved from building to building. There a total of four vacant buildings across from the compound, and he found what he was looking for in the third one. The man had been on the second floor in the corner of the room. Slade breathed in deeply, inhaling the male's scent, making sure it was one he would never forget. It was all the bastard had left behind, but it was enough, for now.

9

They would be coming for her soon, Gypsy knew. She had slipped out of Slade's mind just twenty minutes before, when he was on his way back to check in with the alpha, but before leaving she had read his intent to come straight to her after their meeting. They would have questions, but as hard as she tried to remember where she knew the man from, she couldn't. She had no answers. She knew she needed them if she was going to survive. She needed them to keep her mate safe. However, even though she remembered so many other things in her life, when it came to the man who was terrorizing the compound, she was a blank slate. One thing she did know for certain, though, was that she was not staying in this hospital any longer. She'd had a lot of time to think over the past couple of days, and she knew her place was with her mate.

Jade breezed into the room, setting a backpack down on Gypsy's bed. "These should work for now, Gypsy. It's all I have with me. Chase has put the compound on lock-down until that lunatic is caught."

"Thank you, Jade. I appreciate it. I can't leave the hospital in a gown that opens in the back."

Jade giggled, "That would be a sight! Slade would be so pissed if you flashed the other males in the compound, showing them your panties!"

Gypsy pictured herself walking down the sidewalk in the small town, the back of her gown flapping open for everyone to see her bright blue underwear while Slade glowered at them all, and for the first time in months, she laughed. Not just a small laugh for the benefit of others around her, but a carefree laugh that she felt all of the way down to her toes. She used to laugh all of the time, before she and Sari were taken. By nature, she was a happy, joyful person. Not the quiet, scared one she had become. She wanted to be that person again.

"You better get dressed before the enforcers show up," Jade said, her dark green eyes alight with mirth. "I am so proud of you, Gypsy. Leaving the hospital is a big step, but I believe it is one you are ready to make. I know accepting a mate into your life will be difficult." Placing her hand on Gypsy's arm, Jade looked at her seriously now. "If you need me, Gypsy, all you have to do is reach out to me. I will always be here for you."

I know, Gypsy responded, letting the words drift into the other woman's mind, instead of saying them out loud.

Grabbing the backpack, she went to the bathroom to change. Opening it, she found a brush and a small makeup bag sitting on top. She grinned when she pulled out a matching bright red bra and panty set that still had the tags on them. They were followed by a pair of black leggings and a beautiful multi-colored shirt that was snug in the bodice, but flared out at the waist to settle at her thighs. At the bottom of the bag was a pair of stylish black boots with a small heel. The outfit was perfect, exactly something she would have picked for herself, and everything seemed to be in her size, except the boots. They were half a size too big, but they would work.

Hearing voices in the other room, Gypsy donned the outfit and made quick use of the brush and makeup before placing it back in the bag and zipping it closed. Her heart was fluttering, and it was hard to get her emotions under control. This would be the first time Slade saw her in something besides that dreadful hospital gown. What would he think? Not only that, but what would he say when he found out she had made the decision to leave the hospital? She hoped he would accept her in his home, but if not, she would manage. Gypsy had also decided it was time to take back control of her life. She wanted her mate's support, but she would do it without it if she had to. After one last look in the mirror, she took a deep breath, held her head high, and opened the door.

The first thing Gypsy saw was Slade standing in front of the window. His hands were shoved in his front pockets, his shoulders slightly slumped, as he looked out over the gardens below. She was aware of others in the room, but her eyes never left her mate. He was hers, as she was his. The other half of each other's soul. She had known about shifters before meeting Trace in The Dungeon. The book her mother had given her talked about them, and it discussed the mate bond vaguely, but it did not go into detail about what it entailed. She had learned more about it from Trace when he fought daily to get back to Jade.

She had thought the idea of the mate bond was beautiful. Having one person to love and cherish, one person who was a part of you, for the rest of your lives, was a dream for most. Now, it was reality for her.

As if sensing her presence, Slade turned from the window to face her. She watched as his eyes widened and his nostrils flared. His gaze slowly slid down her body and then back up, a deep growl escaping his throat. Gypsy caught her breath as he took a step toward her, but then seemed to catch himself, stopping and clenching his hands tightly into fists.

You like? She asked the question softly in his mind, afraid to voice it out loud.

I fucking love, came the quick response, followed by another low growl. *Mine.*

"Gypsy, we need to talk to you about the man who took a shot at Slade." The alpha's voice reminded Gypsy that she and Slade were not alone. A quick glance around the room showed Chase, Jade, and one other male she didn't recognize. "This is Bran, my beta. If you aren't comfortable with him being in on this discussion, he can wait in the hall."

Remembering her promise to herself to be the woman she used to be, not the scared one she had become, Gypsy shook her head, "No, he can stay. If he is your beta, then you and Slade trust him. That means I can as well."

Chase nodded, "Yes, you can. As Slade's mate, you are a part of this pack, Gypsy, which means you are under my protection."

"Which also means you are my alpha, and Bran is my beta," Gypsy replied. Walking over to them, she kneeled before Chase and bared her neck. "I accept your generous offer of protection, and I am honored to be a part of your pack, Alpha."

Feeling Chase's hand on the top of her head, Gypsy smiled at the push of energy from him, instantly calming her wayward emotions. "When you are ready, we will have a ceremony announcing your mating and welcoming you to the pack. Until then, know you already are a part of us, and your mating is approved."

Gypsy raised her head and smiled. "Thank you, Alpha."

Chase smiled, letting his hand trail down to cup her cheek. *Why can't my mate be more like you?*

Gypsy caught the words that flitted briefly through his mind, and the guilt that followed. Smiling gently, she responded, *Because she wouldn't be the woman you want, the woman you love, if she was. Everything about her attracts you to her. Her loyalty to her team, her love for her children and determination to keep them safe above all else, her will to survive everything she has been through and become the person she is today. Her rejection is killing you right now, but try and focus on her reason for that rejection.*

We would be stronger together, Chase growled in frustration. *I would fight with her if she would let me.*

Did you ever think that maybe, just maybe, she doesn't let you because she is afraid of losing you? The impression I get from you is that she is a strong woman, always in control, always fighting for what she believes in. But, always losing what is most important to her. The first man she cared for, both of her children. Maybe she is afraid of losing you, too? So, she fights to get rid of the one thing that could take you from her. The General. After he is gone, she will feel safe enough to allow you to claim her.

Chase's eyes narrowed as he contemplated her words.

You are strong, Gypsy. You don't push your mate away right now while we track down and fight the man who is trying to kill him.

Gypsy covered the alpha's hand that still rested against her cheek with her own. Squeezing it, she whispered, *That is only because I am not as strong as your mate.*

His eyes widening slightly in understanding, Chase replied out loud gruffly, "Thank you for that, Gypsy." Leaning down, he helped her to her feet before looking at Slade. "Your mate is wise beyond her years, my friend. The Gods have chosen well for you."

As they have for you. Gypsy savored her alpha's look of gratitude before walking over to sit in the chair next to Slade. Slade's hand rested on her shoulder, and she covered it with her own. As she did, she caught the glimpse of a blonde haired, blue-eyed woman, and a touch of love and deep sadness from him, and then it was gone. Who was she? Someone very special to Slade, but Gypsy also got the impression the woman was not around anymore, and hadn't been for some time. It was as if when Slade thought of her, he was thinking of a past life.

"You are safe here, Gypsy," Chase said, as he crossed over and shut the door for privacy. "We need to know anything and everything that you can tell us about the sniper who is targeting the pack. Whatever you tell us now will not leave this room."

Gypsy's hand tightened on Slade's nervously, her gaze going from Chase, to Bran, to Jade, then back to Chase. "I don't remember him, Chase. I'm sorry. I have tried and tried, and even though I feel like I should know who he is, I just can't remember."

"You're blocking it." Jade moved forward and knelt by

Gypsy, resting a hand gently on hers over the light pink cast. "You don't want to remember him."

"Yes, I do," Gypsy insisted. "I don't want him to hurt anyone else."

"I know," Jade whispered. "You could never harm anyone, Gypsy. Someone told me once that I'm a healer, not a fighter, and I think that is the case for you, too."

"I don't heal people," Gypsy protested. "That is beyond my abilities."

"You bring them back from death's door. If that isn't healing, then I don't know what is."

Gypsy looked down into Jade's eyes, so full of compassion and understanding. "Not always," she admitted quietly. "There was one person I wasn't able to bring back." Tears of regret slipped down her cheeks as she remembered that cold, dark night so long ago. "It was raining," she whispered, a shudder rippling through her, "and it was so dark. The moon was hidden, and very few stars lit the night sky. I remember it clearly because I am able to draw energy from the moon to help strengthen me if I need it. That night, there was none. I just kept thinking, maybe if the moon had been out, maybe then I could have saved him." Slade moved to stand directly behind Gypsy, silently running a hand down her long, soft hair. She leaned back against his chest, sighing as she felt his support and strength filling her. "I had just arrived to New Orleans the day before with some friends. Against my mother's wishes, the three of us were going on spring break together. It was early morning, around 2 a.m. I wanted to go back to the hotel to sleep, but Kelly and Nicole weren't ready yet. They were having fun, but I was exhausted. I decided to head back on my own. The streets were crowded, so I thought it would be safe."

"What happened?" Slade asked, lightly stroking her shoulder with his thumb.

"There was this young boy, no more than ten or eleven years old. He was a beggar with filthy, torn clothes, and shoulder-length shaggy hair." He was a handsome boy, with some of the greenest eyes she had ever seen. His face was pale, with a smattering of brown freckles covering his nose. "He made the mistake of trying to steal a wallet from one of the men on the street, right in front of where I was walking. The man grabbed him and threw him in the alleyway next to the street, leaving without looking back. The poor little boy hit his head on the corner of a dumpster, cutting it deeply. I knew he was dying. I felt it." Raising her gaze to Chase's, she whispered, "I tried to help him, but no matter what I did, I couldn't connect with him. To bring them back, I have to be able to connect, but I just couldn't."

"You weren't meant to," Jade said simply.

Gypsy nodded, clasping her hands together tightly in her lap. "I realize that now. A book that is handed down from generation to generation in my family states that I can only save those who are meant to be saved. But that night, with that little boy, almost broke me. I have this wonderful gift, powerful beyond anything I have ever known, and I could not help him."

"How many others have you helped? How many other lives have you saved?"

"Four, including Xavier," Gypsy admitted.

"Be proud of that, Gypsy. Be happy that you were able to save them. I know their families are." Looking into

Jade's eyes, Gypsy nodded, reaching up to wipe away her tears. Jade was right. She was not meant to save that small boy, no matter how much she wished the outcome had been different. It was time to face it, and move on. Hadn't she just told Xavier that she could only save the ones that were meant to be saved?

"If you will allow me to," Jade inquired softly, "I have the ability to merge with you and see what you have seen in the past. Maybe, together, we can find out who this man is that you can't remember?"

Did she want Jade in her mind? Did she want the kind, gentle woman to be exposed to the terror and torture she had gone through in The Dungeon? "I promise you, I will not share anything with the others that you don't want me to."

"No, it's not that," Gypsy said when she felt Slade's hands tighten on her shoulders. "I have nothing to hide. I just don't want you to have to relive what I went through, Jade."

"Trust me, I will be fine. I've been through hell myself and survived."

The truth was there in Jade's eyes for Gypsy to see. Taking a deep breath, she finally agreed. "Let's get it done, then." When Slade made a move to remove his hands from her shoulders, Gypsy reached up and grasped them tightly with her own. *No, please. I need your strength.*

She shivered when she felt Slade's lips touch the top of her head. *Always.*

Gypsy closed her eyes and lowered her head, still holding tightly to Slade. She could do this. She was strong and brave, just like Chase's mate. *Yes,* she felt Jade whisper into her mind, *You are very strong. Now just relax. First, I want you to take me back to the time you were held captive.* A shudder racked Gypsy's body, fear swamping her. She didn't want to go back to The Dungeon. There was only terror and death there. *You are safe, my friend. Your mate is here, as is your alpha. No one will ever harm you again. Trust me.*

I do. Slowly, Gypsy allowed herself to drift back to a time she would rather forget. Now that she had her memory back, she wondered why she had fought to retrieve the memories in the first place. They were full of nothing but pain and despair.

For close to half an hour, Jade stayed in Gypsy's mind, reliving the past with her; the agony, the torture, the complete loss of hope. Gypsy's shoulders slumped and her body was racked with sobs as she was forced to endure the memories along with her friend. Finally, when she was sure she could not handle anymore, she heard Jade's voice *You did a wonderful job, Gypsy. I think I have everything I need. Now, show me what happened today.*

Gypsy stiffened in fear, but forged on, determined to find out who wanted her back bad enough to try and kill not only her mate, but other members of the pack. It was not long before she had her answer. Her eyes springing open, she gasped the name of the one man who instilled terror in her like no other, "Titus!" Fear engulfed her, and a scream tore from her throat. "No…no! Slade!"

She felt strong arms pulling her from the chair and holding her close as her mate gently rubbed a hand up and down her back. "Ssshhh, Gypsy. No one is ever going to hurt you again. That bastard will not get near you."

"Titus thinks I'm his," Gypsy moaned, hugging Slade tightly to her. "He used to hurt me, Slade. He hit me over and over again, and allowed his men to beat me, too. He is the one who broke my arm because I tried to feed Trace when they were starving him. He said the food was a gift from him, one that he had to sneak from his boss, so he was teaching me a lesson."

"Did he…"

Slade left the rest unsaid, but she knew what he wanted to hear. His body shook slightly, and he buried his face in her neck while he waited for her response. "No, Titus never actually forced himself on me. He wanted to, but he said he was waiting. He had paid Perez a lot of money for me, but he could not actually have me until Perez tired of my sister. Once that happened, Titus said we were leaving. He wanted to take me somewhere else to live, far away from Perez because he didn't trust him. But he never actually told me where."

"We need to call RARE in for help on this, Chase," Bran said quietly. "We need their expertise."

Chase cursed softly. "I actually have a call into Angel now, but I haven't heard back."

"That's because they've gone dark."

"What the hell does that mean, Jade?" Chase demanded.

Gypsy raised her head from Slade's chest to look over at Jade. She obviously knew something the others in the room did not, but she was struggling with herself on whether or not she should say anything. "It means that we have no way of contacting them for help right now. We are on our own."

"Where the hell are they?" Chase roared.

Gypsy pressed herself closer to Slade as she waited for

Jade's answer. "I'm not supposed to tell anyone because it could compromise their mission."

"You can tell me," Chase growled. "As your alpha, I am ordering you to."

"That's not fair, Chase," Jade whispered. "Angel is my mother. Don't put me in this position."

"They've gone after Storm," Gypsy interjected. "They got a lead on where the General may be holding her right now, and they had to act fast before they lose her." At Jade's gasp of dismay, Gypsy shrugged apologetically, "This way is better, Jade. You didn't betray your mother or your alpha. And you were broadcasting your thoughts. I couldn't help but pick up on them." At Chase's deep snarl, Gypsy turned to him. "You have to let your mate do what she needs to do, Chase. Be there to support her, but don't demand her obedience in anything. You are both alphas, so any kind of relationship will be difficult. But, if you don't do this, you will lose her."

Chase's eyes flashed wolf, then back again several times before he turned and walked out of the room, Bran on his heels. Gypsy could feel anger and frustration emanating from him in waves, and she didn't blame him, but he had to get control of his emotions if he and Angel were going to survive their mating.

"Thank you," Jade said softly, before she stood and followed them out the door.

Squaring her shoulders, Gypsy stepped back away from Slade and reached for the bag on the bed. "Are you ready?"

"Ready for what?" he asked in confusion.

"To go home," Gypsy responded, tensely waiting for Slade's response. She had thought long and hard about what she would do when she left the hospital. She could have asked Chase for a place to live for now, or she could have asked Jade if she could stay with her. But, the fact of the matter was, she had a mate, and she belonged with him. She knew it would be hard for a human to understand what it meant to be mated, but she was not necessarily human. She was something more. Not only did she know what it meant, but she welcomed it. It would not be easy, but she and Slade would figure it out together. Eventually, love would come with the mate bond. At least, she hoped it would for Slade. She was already feeling the slight stirrings of something herself, and hoped it would continue to grow. According to what Trace told her, whenever the bond kicked in, love was always close behind it.

"You want to come home with me?"

She wanted to do more than just go home with him. "Yes. Where else would I go?" Deciding she was done waiting for his approval, Gypsy left the room, hoping he would follow. Stopping to see her sister on the way out, she walked quickly over to the bed and kissed Sari softly on her cheek. "I will be back soon to see you, sweetheart. When you are ready, I will bring you home with us." Sari stirred slightly, then sighed as she snuggled deeper into the covers. Gypsy hated to leave her, but she knew her sister was not ready to go beyond the hospital walls yet. To her, they represented safety. Not only that, but Sari needed help and guidance that Gypsy could not give her. Promising herself that she would visit frequently, Gypsy walked out into the hall where Slade was waiting. "I'm ready."

10

Slade walked next to Gypsy, his eyes constantly scanning the area around them as they quickly made their way to his apartment. His breathing was labored and his cock rock-hard as he thought about what he wanted to do to his mate when he got her back to his place. He had been shocked when she said she was coming home with him. As much as he wanted her there, he had thought it would be weeks before she even contemplated something like that. Maybe she just wanted a place to sleep. Fuck, he hoped not. He didn't think he could be in the same apartment as Gypsy and not touch her.

He would not claim her. There were too many reasons not to right now, and at the top of that list was Sarah. It wasn't that he was keeping his first wife a secret from Gypsy, so much as he was afraid telling her about Sarah would hurt whatever relationship they were beginning to build. How would Gypsy feel if she found out he had married his first love, forsaking their mate bond? Would she turn him away? He had no idea, but until he found the balls to tell her about Sarah, he would have to keep his fangs to himself. That did not mean, however, that he would be able to keep from making love to her. He had never felt the pure lust he felt for Gypsy with anyone else, not even Sarah. He had loved her unconditionally, and they'd had a good, satisfying sex life, but he had never felt the animal attraction for her that he felt for Gypsy.

"Who is she?" Slade froze at the softly spoken question. Exactly how did she know what he was thinking? If Gypsy could speak to him telepathically, did that mean she could hear his thoughts? Could she read his mind? He hoped not. There were things in his life that he wasn't ready to share with her just yet. "I'm sorry, I didn't mean to pry, but I can tell you loved her very much."

Slade stayed silent until they reached his apartment. Opening the door, he ushered Gypsy inside and shut it behind him, making sure to turn the lock. "She's nobody."

"Slade, that's not true."

"I don't want to talk about her right now." Taking the backpack from Gypsy's hand, he frowned when he felt how light it was. "What's in this thing?"

Gypsy shrugged, "Nothing, really. I don't have anything." Gesturing to the clothes she wore, she said, "All of this came from Jade. She told me she had more she would share with me until I can go shopping."

Stopping abruptly on his way to the bedroom, he growled, "Hell, Gypsy, I'm sorry. I didn't even think about you not having any clothes or shoes. As soon as I can, I will take you to get some things of your own." How could he have forgotten to buy her clothes? His mind had been so consumed with thoughts of how to keep her safe, along with the rest of the pack, that he had forgotten the simplest things his mate needed.

"I haven't had anything of my own for almost a year now," she replied, "a few more days isn't going to make a difference."

He hated to hear that. It was a reminder of the hell she had endured at the hands of a madman. A hell Slade would have done anything to prevent if given the chance. There was nothing he could do about the past, but he would make damn sure no one hurt her again. Tossing the bag on the couch, he crossed the distance that separated them and pulled her into his arms. The moment her lush body sank into his, he realized his mistake. He had thought to give her some time before taking her. He had even given himself a stern lecture while he waited for her to finish checking on her sister in the hospital. There was no doubt in his mind that it would happen, but he could give her a few more days to get to know him first.

"Gypsy," her name was a low groan on his lips as he fought with himself to step back, to separate their bodies and move across the room. But it was a futile effort. When she slipped her arms around his waist and tilted her head back to look at him, he gave in, capturing her mouth with his own. She moaned, pressing fully against him, her nails digging into his back. Sliding his fingers into her thick hair, he growled deeply as he licked at her lips. He loved the way she tasted, like sugar and spice. It was like nothing he had ever tasted before. He could not get enough of her.

Gypsy loosened her hold from around his waist and he felt her small hands grab hold of his shirt and slide it slowly up his body. Slade let go of her mouth just long enough to remove it, before finding her lips again. Slipping his hands slowly down her back, he cupped her ass and pulled her roughly against him. Rubbing his aching cock against her, he cursed at the clothing that separated them. "I need to feel you, sweetheart," he groaned. "I need your soft, sweet skin against mine."

Gypsy put a hand on his chest and pushed gently. *No, fuck no.* She could not make him stop now. She pushed again, and he ground against her one more time before reluctantly letting her go. He would never force his mate to do anything she did not want to do, even if it practically killed him to pull back. Taking one step away from her, then another, he rasped, "I need to get out of here."

"No, you don't," Gypsy whispered. Grasping the bottom of her shirt, she pulled it up over her head to drop it on the floor. Slade lost the ability to think when she toed off her boots, and then slipped her fingers into her leggings and slid them over her slender hips and down her legs, kicking them off.

"Gypsy?" It was a question, but it was also a plea.

"You aren't going anywhere, Slade. I need you."

At those words, Slade could not stop another low growl from escaping. Quickly closing the distance between them, he scooped Gypsy up in his arms and hurried to his bedroom. Kicking the door shut behind them, he laid her down gently on the bed before stepping back to look at her. She was so beautiful. Her long, brown hair fanned out around her on the pillow, her dark eyes sparkled with desire, and her soft skin begged for his touch. His gaze drifted from the red wisps of lace barely covering her full breasts, down her soft stomach, to more lace that stood between him and what he wanted most.

He slowly raked his gaze over her body, from top to bottom, and then back up again. Their eyes caught and held, as his hands went to the button on his jeans. "Are you sure, Gypsy? Once these come off, I won't be able to stop."

Her eyes left his and trailed down his body to where his hands rested. "Yes," she breathed. "I want to feel your hands on me. I want you inside of me."

Slade could not hold back any longer. Undoing the button, he quickly slid off his jeans, and his boxer briefs with them. He watched as Gypsy stared at his thick erection, slowly licking her lips. He wanted to feel those soft, pink lips wrapped around his dick. He wanted to pump into her mouth, watching her take all of him. But his desire to bury himself deep inside his mate won out and he climbed on the bed, resting on his knees beside her legs. Letting his gaze wander over her again, he could not stop himself from snarling, "Mine."

"Yes," she panted softly, "as you are mine."

Reaching out, Slade softly skimmed his fingers along her thigh, up over the silky skin on her belly, to the top of a breast. She was so damn stunning. Letting one of his claws emerge, he deftly sliced the front of her bra open, chuckling at the gasp that emerged from Gypsy. He peeled the lacey cups back from her beautiful breasts, cupping one of them in his palm. He groaned when it filled his hand perfectly. Lowering his head, he licked around the nipple, then sucked it gently into his mouth, before nipping at it. "Slade!" Gypsy cried out, sliding her fingers into his hair and clasping him to her. Moving to her other breast, he gave it the same attention he had given the first as he reached down and cut the panties from her. Retracting his claw, he slowly slid his hand over her mound and slipped a finger inside her.

Slade groaned as he moved up to capture her soft cry with his mouth. Rubbing her clit with his thumb, he began pushing his finger in and out of her, adding one more after a few thrusts. Gypsy moaned, pulling her mouth from his and flinging her head back, crying out as she arched into his touch. "Oh, God, Slade!" He continued his onslaught, loving the sounds of pleasure coming from her. "Slade!"

A scream tore from her throat as she came, and Slade watched in shock as a bright glow emanated from her body. Gypsy opened her eyes, eyes that glowed a dark golden-brown, and panted, "My turn." Pushing him onto his back, she straddled his legs and leaned down to kiss him. His body shuddered as she grasped his aching cock in her hand. She began to stroke his thick length as she slipped her tongue into his mouth, tangling it with his.

Slade groaned as he rotated his hips, thrusting his cock into her hand. It felt so damn good. There was one thing that would feel better, though. Grasping her hips, he pulled her up until her moist folds slid over his cock. Lifting her slightly, he groaned as he slowly lowered her onto his straining erection, encasing him in her hot wetness.

Gypsy sat up, her hands on his chest, and slowly raised herself up, then back down. He watched her tongue slip out to moisten her lips as she tilted her head back. Gypsy's long hair flowed down her back, her eyes were slightly closed, and the noises coming from her as she rode him drove him wild. His fangs punched through his gums, and he tightened his hold on her hips, guiding her faster as he pushed deeper inside her. A thin sheen of sweat coated Gypsy's body, and her beautiful breasts moved up and down in sync with his thrusts.

Making sure they stayed connected, Slade flipped her over onto her back. Bending down, he took one of her hard nipples in his mouth, scraping it with his fangs, and then soothing the sting with his tongue. Gypsy called his name as he continued to move deep inside her. Letting go of one breast, he quickly found the other one, reveling in the soft cries coming from his mate.

"Slade, please," Gypsy panted, pushing up into him, "I'm so close."

Slade let go of her breast and looked into her still glowing eyes. Tangling his hand into her hair, he grasped it tightly and tilted her head to the side, exposing her neck to his hungry gaze. Leaning in, he began to lick and nibble his way down the sensitive skin on her neck. Stopping at the soft hollow between her neck and shoulder, he gently sucked the skin into his mouth, before lightly scraping his fangs over to her shoulder. He wanted to mark her, to claim her as his mate. He wanted to sink his teeth deep into her shoulder so that everyone would know that she belonged to him. Opening his mouth, he placed his fangs on her shoulder as he pumped deep inside her. It would be so easy to make her his.

Gypsy cried out, dragging her nails down his back and digging them into his ass as she came. Snarling, Slade slammed into her two more times before he spilled inside her. Just as his jaw started to tighten on her tender flesh, an image of Sarah ran through his mind. With a roar, he pulled his teeth away from Gypsy's shoulder and buried his head in her neck breathing heavily. More images of

Sarah swamped him, and he fought to block them out. He did not want Gypsy to see them, and he was sure she could.

"Slade?" Gypsy's small voice broke through the mixture of emotions swirling through him. She placed a soft kiss on the side of his head, gently stroking her hand down his back. "Talk to me, Slade, please."

"I can't," he grunted, "dammit, Gypsy, I just can't."

"If you don't, then we aren't going to get past this," she whispered, "and I really do not think that is an option for mates, Slade."

Slade swallowed hard, another shudder racking his body. He didn't know what to say. What if she left him?

"What was her name?" Gypsy asked softly, still hesitantly stroking his back.

Slade tightened his fist in her hair, fighting tears that threatened to break free. "Sarah," he rasped finally. "Her name was Sarah."

"And you loved her?"

"Yes," he admitted. "I did."

"Who was she to you?" The question was voiced quietly, but the hand on his back had stilled. He could feel her starting to withdraw from him, and that was why he had not wanted to have this conversation. Not yet. Not until their relationship was stronger.

"She was my wife."

"Your wife?" Gypsy asked in confusion, slowly pulling away from him and sitting up. Grabbing the sheet from the bottom of the bed, she held it up to cover her breasts. "But, I thought shifters only got one mate? You said I am yours? I know I am. I feel it, too."

"They do," Slade agreed roughly, resting his forehead

on the pillow in front of him. Shit, how could he explain this to her without losing her? "Not all shifters find their mates, Gypsy. Some can look for years and never find them, so they choose to live their lives alone. Some fall in love and marry."

"Even knowing their mate could be out there somewhere waiting for them?"

"Yes," he said shortly.

Gypsy rose from the bed, wrapping the sheet snuggly around her. "Where is she?"

"She died years ago." Clutching tightly to the pillow, he lay in silence for several minutes, trying to collect his thoughts. "I'm sorry, Gypsy," he finally said. "I should have waited for you, but…" Slade froze when he realized that he was alone. Lifting his head, he slowly turned around to look at the empty room. "Shit," he hissed as he sat up and threw the pillow. "That went well." Cursing loudly when he heard the soft click of the lock on the front door moments later, he jumped out of bed and ran to the living room, but he was too late. She was gone.

11

When she left the apartment, Gypsy had no specific destination in mind. All she knew was that she needed to get out of there. She had no idea what to think. It was obvious that Slade was still in love with his deceased wife. Gypsy had known that he was about to bite her, to claim her as his, and she had welcomed it. Then, images of a pretty, young woman with long, straight, blonde hair and some of the bluest eyes she'd ever seen had come between them.

It had not been Gypsy's intention to read his thoughts. She never tried to get inside anyone's head, but sometimes things slipped through. This time Slade had been projecting his thoughts so loudly that she was unable to block them out.

A few minutes later, Gypsy found herself in front of the hospital, the only place in the compound that she was familiar with. Sighing, she decided she would go inside and check on her sister before trying to figure out what to do next. Did she go back to Slade's apartment? Did she stay in her room at the hospital? She was so confused.

"Gypsy?" Jade's soft voice came to her from the top of the stairs.

Glancing up, Gypsy gave her a weak smile. "Hi Jade. I came to look in on Sari." It was partly true. It may not have been her original reason for coming, but it was the decision she had just made.

Gypsy could tell Jade suspected there was more to her surprise return, but the other woman did not ask. "Come in out of the cold," she said, motioning to the front doors. "You are going to freeze out here."

Looking back toward the apartments, Gypsy saw Slade standing out in front of them watching her. He wore a pair of jeans, but nothing else. Even his feet were bare. He did not make an attempt to move in her direction. It seemed as if he were waiting for something, with his hands resting on his hips, and his head cocked to the side.

Making her way silently down the stairs, Jade came to stand beside Gypsy. "He won't leave until he knows you are safely inside the hospital," she said quietly. "If your intention is to have some time apart, I suggest you come with me now."

Tearing her gaze away from Slade, Gypsy turned and trudged up the stairs. It was not what she wanted to do. She wanted to turn back around and run to her mate. She wanted to take him in her arms and tell him everything was going to be all right. That no matter what, she was not going anywhere, and they would work things out. Maybe he didn't love her now, but she knew he cared for her, and love would come eventually. Her heart was already starting to open to him. One day, his would for her as well.

When Gypsy reached the front entrance, she placed her hand on the door and turned back one last time to look at Slade, but he was gone. A tear escaped and slid down her cheek unnoticed. Jade was wrong. She had not made it safely inside yet, but her mate was nowhere to be found.

A soft sob catching in her throat, Gypsy turned and ran through the front doors. Did she even have a chance? Would Slade ever love her like he did Sarah? Could she stay with him if he could never feel more for her? How could she leave? From what she knew, mates could not stand to be apart for very long. Even now, without the mating bite, the pull between them was strong. She wanted to be with him, and had to fight the urge to turn back.

Stopping in front of her sister's room, Gypsy knocked lightly on the open door. Sari was sitting up in bed watching television. She smiled when she saw Gypsy, and quickly shut it off. That smile turned into a frown when she saw Gypsy was no longer wearing one of the hospital gowns they had both worn since they arrived. Nibbling on her bottom lip, Sari asked nervously, "Where were you, Gypsy? I wanted to come see you earlier, but they said you weren't in your room."

Gypsy had asked the staff to allow her to be the one to tell Sari that she was leaving the hospital. She did not expect them to deliver that kind of news to her sister, especially when she had no idea how Sari was going to respond. Smiling gently, Gypsy walked in and sat on the side of the bed. "I've been at Slade's," she admitted.

"Slade's?" Sari questioned in confusion. "Who's Slade?"

That was when Gypsy realized that she and her sister had not had a chance to sit down and talk. At first it was because of Gypsy's memory loss. Since she was unable to remember the young girl, she'd had no idea what to say to her. Once she finally regained her memory, Sari had closed in on herself and spent most of her time in bed following her minor breakdown. Now Gypsy wondered just how much she should tell her. There was a time when the two had talked about almost anything…anything except Gypsy's gifts. That was something she had not been allowed to share with anyone in the past, but maybe now it was time. She trusted her sister with her life, and she was so tired of carrying her burdens alone. That was exactly what her abilities had become to her over the past few years; burdens.

In the beginning, Gypsy's powers were magical and fun. She used to love to sneak in and out of people's minds just to see what they were thinking. Well, most people. Some minds were scarier than others. She had learned fast to leave instantly when she touched the dark sludge of hatred and evil that was alive in some. When she got older, she became more wary about others finding out about her abilities and began to heed her mother's advice. She became better at hiding the things she could do, but it did not stop her from helping those in need if she could.

Deciding it was time to share everything with Sari, Gypsy stood and kicked off her boots before sliding onto the bed and leaning back against the pillows beside her sister. "There are so many things you don't know about me, Sari," she started slowly. "Things I always wanted to tell you, but Mom was afraid of what might happen to me, to all of us really, if I did."

"Well, you can tell me now."

Hesitating slightly, Gypsy said, "Growing up, you always knew we had different fathers. I loved our Papa so much, but he wasn't my biological father." When Sari nodded, Gypsy continued, "My dad was a very special man. He had gifts that not a lot of people have. Gifts that he passed down to me."

Sari's eyebrows rose, a look of suspicion in her eyes. "Like what?"

"I can do things, Sari. Things you wouldn't believe."

"Are you going to tell me how you turn into a glow worm sometimes at night? Because I already know about that."

Gypsy looked at Sari in surprise. "You've seen me?"

Sari flushed as she looked away. "You would leave the house sometimes really late at night. I have always had trouble sleeping, so I started following you. I just wanted to see where you went."

"You saw me dancing under the moon?" Gypsy guessed softly.

"You were so beautiful," Sari admitted, a slight apology in her voice. "I couldn't seem to stay away. You would start to sort of glow, getting brighter and brighter, and then you would say things. It was like you were talking to the moon and stars, and they were responding."

"Why didn't you ever ask me about it?"

Sari shrugged, leaning closer and resting her head on Gypsy's shoulder. "You didn't want me to know. If you did, you would have told me."

"Not true," Gypsy said, laying her cheek on the top of Sari's head.

"No?"

"I always wanted to tell you. We never kept secrets from each other. But, Mom wouldn't let me." Sighing, Gypsy told her the whole truth. "People used to think my father was a witch. He was killed by hunters, and Mom was always afraid that they were hunting us."

She heard Sari gasp softly, and then she whispered, "I'm so sorry, Gypsy." They sat in silence for several minutes before Sari asked, "Do you hate me, Gypsy? Is that why you don't come to see me very often?"

"What?" Gypsy pulled away from Sari, and placing a finger under her sister's chin, she raised her head until their eyes met. "There was one reason, and one reason only that I never came to see you before, Sari Elizabeth, and it most definitely was not because I hate you."

"Then why?" Sari's chin trembled as she fought back tears.

"Sari, something happened to me when we were rescued, and I lost my memory. I honestly had no idea who I was, let alone who you were. I have never, ever hated you. Why would you think that?"

"Because it's my fault we were taken. Dad and Mom died, and you were hurt, all because of me." Sobs tore from Sari's throat, tears falling from her eyes.

"Who told you that?"

"Philip did. He said he wanted me, so he eliminated anyone he thought would get in his way. He killed our parents, and then he kept you locked up in that horrible place. He told me that every time I did something that he didn't like, he would hurt you. I always messed up. I could never make him happy. I'm so sorry, Gypsy. Please don't hate me!"

Gypsy enfolded the devastated girl into her arms, crooning softly to her. "I could never hate you, sweetheart. I love you so much, and none of this was because of you. Nothing that happened was in any way your fault. Philip Perez was a sadistic bastard. An evil, cold-hearted son of a bitch who liked to prey on young girls and feed off the fear of others. Nothing you could have done would have ever made him happy."

Gypsy rocked her sister back and forth in her arms for a long time before Sari finally calmed down, her head resting on Gypsy's chest. Lightly touching the cast on Gypsy's left arm, she asked, "Did he do this to you because of me?"

"No," Gypsy promised, "this had nothing to do with you. Actually, Philip didn't break my arm. Titus did."

"Titus?"

"Yes. He was one of Philip's henchmen. He would come down into The Dungeon to torture all of the prisoners. I was no exception." A shiver ran up Gypsy's spine as she remembered the beatings she had endured at the hands of not only Titus, but the other guards. There had been so much pain and suffering for so long. "Titus used to bring me extra food sometimes, which wasn't saying much. They did not like to feed us often. They needed to keep their prisoners weak." At Sari's gasp of dismay, Gypsy placed a soft kiss on the top of her head before continuing. "One time I tried to feed Trace some of the food he brought me. Titus found out and punished me severely. The broken arm was the worst of it, though. He said I was his. That he had paid

Perez a lot of money for me, so he could do whatever he wanted to me."

"What?" Sari cried, raising shocked eyes to Gypsy's. "He owned you?"

Lifting her chin slightly in defiance, Gypsy said, "He thought he did, but he was wrong. No one owns me."

Sari's lower lip trembled as she whispered raggedly, "I missed you so much, Gypsy."

"Me too, my love. Me too."

Laying her head back down on Gypsy's chest, Sari spoke so quietly Gypsy had to strain to hear her. "They told me I lost my baby." As far as Gypsy knew, that was the first time Sari had spoken of the infant she miscarried. "Philip killed him. I would have loved him, Gypsy. I would have loved my baby, no matter what."

"I know, Sari." It broke Gypsy's heart that her sister was suffering, and there was nothing she could do about it. She should be hanging out with friends right now, talking about boys and what shoes to buy next. Instead, Sari was hiding in a hospital room, afraid to face the world after walking through the fires of hell.

Gypsy held her sister as she cried for the loss of her baby. The poor girl had lost everything. Her parents, her baby, her home, her innocence. But, she survived. She had lived, and no matter what, Gypsy vowed to help her move on and learn to love life again. After a while, only soft sniffles could be heard.

Trying to take Sari's mind off of her pain, Gypsy whispered, "I met someone, Sis."

After a moment of silence, she heard, "Slade?"

"Yes." Lowering the hospital bed down slightly, Gypsy settled back against the pillows holding her sister close.

"He's an enforcer for the White River Wolves here at the compound." Sticking to her vow from before to always be honest with Sari from now on, she continued, "He's my mate."

"Mate?"

"Kind of like a soul mate, but so much more." Sari sighed as she snuggled closer. "I'm going to tell you some things, Sari. Things that you have to promise not to tell anyone. It could put some wonderful people in danger if you do."

"I promise." There was no hesitation in Sari's voice, only acceptance. Her little sister had been forced to grow up so fast, and Gypsy hated Philip Perez for it.

"Some of the people of this compound are different," she began softly. "They are magical, powerful beings."

"Like you?"

"Like me, but so much more. They can do things that I can't. They have the ability to shift into wolves, and I even heard something about a bear and a fox." She expected shock and denial from Sari, but she got neither.

"And panthers," Sari said quietly.

Gypsy stiffened in surprise. It was obvious her sister knew about Trace, and there was only one way she could have found out. "You overheard Philip and his men talking, didn't you?"

"Yes," Sari agreed, a shiver running through her body. "They were experimenting with Trace. Seeing exactly how far they could go before they killed him. Philip didn't want him dead, but he told his men to push him to his limits. I remember one of them said he didn't understand how Trace could still be alive after everything they'd done to him."

Tears filled Gypsy's eyes as she remembered watching each and every one of those torture sessions. The struggle with life and death had been a daily constant in Trace's life. "I do," she told Sari. "Trace is strong, and courageous. He wanted to free us, to get us away from that place. And he wanted to come home to Jade. Mates will do anything for each other, Sari. They are the other half of one another's soul. Without one, the other loses the will to go on. Trace had to come home to Jade. There was no other choice."

"So that means Slade is the other half of your soul?"

Gypsy took a moment to respond. Closing her eyes, she pictured Slade; so strong, loyal, and brave. "Yes," she replied. "He is. I feel it, deep inside. I know, no matter what, he will always be there for me. He will always protect me."

"Even from someone like Philip? What if someone kidnaps us again? What if…?"

"Hush," Gypsy whispered, rubbing her back gently, "Hush, baby. Heaven forbid that would ever happen. But, if it did, Slade would hunt to the ends of the Earth for us, because I am his, and that's what mates do."

"Do you think maybe I have a mate out there, too?" The soft question was spoken with both trepidation and a hint of hope. "Do you think someday, someone will want me like that? Even after what Philip did to me?"

"I know someone is out there who will love you, care for you, and treat you the way you deserve to be treated someday, Sari. He may be human, he may be other, but I know he is out there."

"How do you know?"

"I have gifts of my own, remember?" Tilting Sari's

head up so she could look at her, Gypsy grinned as she leaned down and gently rubbed their noses together. "Trust me, little sister, your future is very bright and full of joy. You will get past everything that has happened. You will move on. It will take time, but it will happen. I promise you." She would do everything in her power to keep that promise.

Sari's eyes filled with tears, and one slipped out. "I hope so. It is so hard right now, Gypsy."

Sari laid her head back down, and Gypsy tightened her arms around her. It was not long before soft snores filled the silence. After Sari fell asleep, Gypsy continued to hold her close, because she needed that comfort as well. She needed to know that somebody loved her, and cared for her. That they needed her, like Sari did. The minutes stretched into hours, and when she finally glanced toward the window, she was shocked to see that it was pitch black outside. The clock on the wall read 3 a.m.

Gypsy slipped out of the bed and used the buttons on a remote to lower it down all of the way so Sari would be more comfortable. Pulling the covers up, she gave her sister one last kiss on her brow before leaving. Walking down the hall, she paused outside her old room, but knew that was not where she belonged. Waving to the nurse at the front counter, she left the building. Lost in thought, Gypsy walked slowly down the front stairs, stopping to look up at the sliver of moon that showed from behind some dark clouds. She didn't hear the man behind her until it was too late. "I've missed you," a terrifying voice from her past said before a hand covered her mouth and she felt a small prick in the side of her neck.

12

After Gypsy left his apartment, Slade made it outside in time to see her standing in front of the hospital talking with Jade. She'd turned to look at him, and he had thought maybe she would come back. When she turned back around and walked up the stairs, he waited just long enough to make sure she made it to the doors, before backing out of sight. He watched as she looked in his direction one more time, before going into the building. Fighting the urge to follow her, he cursed beneath his breath and stomped back up to his apartment. Quickly changing into sweats and a tee-shirt, he grabbed his duffle bag and left again.

Slade spent the rest of the day in the gym, pounding the piss out of one of the punching bags hanging in a corner, and then taking on Chase when he showed up. Both men had a lot of aggression to let out, and once they finished in the gym, they shifted and ran the perimeter of the compound, checking for signs of an intruder. Finding none, Slade finally went back to his apartment, hoping Gypsy had shown up. When he didn't see her, he called the hospital and was told she was resting with her sister. He was not happy, but knowing she was safe, he decided to try and get some sleep himself. Unfortunately, he was unable to without Gypsy by his side.

Several hours later, Slade looked at the clock again before slamming his fist into the pillow. It was early morning, and he had spent the night alone, wide awake. This was not the way it was supposed to be. His mate had been in his apartment, in his bed. He should have kept her there. Instead, he once again managed to fuck things up and made her run.

Rolling out of bed, Slade dressed in record time. He had never thought he would find his mate, and now that he had her, he would be a fool to let her slip away. Gypsy stirred things in him, things long forgotten. Instead of fighting them, he was going to grab on tightly and never let go. Grabbing his coat, Slade left the apartment and practically ran to the hospital. He needed to see Gypsy now. He wanted to hold her in his arms and tell her how he felt.

Scaling the stairs two at a time, he was through the front doors and down the hallway in an instant. Stopping at Sari's door, he glanced around in confusion when he did not see Gypsy with her. Leaving the girl asleep, he turned and stalked back down the hall to Gypsy's old room. Maybe she had decided to stay alone last night. Opening the door, Slade took in the vacant room. The sheets on the bed were undisturbed, and there was no sign of anyone being there recently.

Something was not right. He could feel it. His mate

was gone. Rushing out of the room, he ran to the front counter. "Where's Gypsy?" he demanded loudly.

The nurse at the desk jumped, lifting a frightened gaze to him. "Gypsy? I haven't seen her since she left last night," she stammered.

"Who did she leave with?" he demanded.

"Slade?" Slade turned to see Jade striding toward him, her green eyes wide with concern. "What's going on?"

"Did Gypsy stay with you last night?" he asked, praying she had.

Slowly, Jade shook her head. "No. I left here late in the evening, and she was in with Sari."

A cold chill ran through him, dark and foreboding, followed by a low, steady growl that began to build deep in his throat. Unable to control his wolf, he felt his fangs extend and his claws begin to emerge as he growled, "Where is my mate?"

"Get Chase on the phone, now," Josie ordered as she walked up and threw a clipboard on the counter. "Slade, you have to calm down. You are not helping matters."

His dark eyes going wolf, Slade turned on her. "My mate is fucking missing!" he roared. "Don't tell me to calm down!"

"Are you talking about Gypsy?" the soft, timid voice came from down the hall. "Is my sister missing?"

Slade's eyes connected with the wide, frightened ones coming slowly toward him, and he fought to get his wolf back under control. The child had been through enough, she did not need to see Slade shift in front of everyone. "I will find her," he promised roughly, struggling to make his fangs recede. "I will bring her back home to you, Sari."

Slade was aware of Chase walking through the doors

and striding in his direction as Sari stopped in front of him. "I know you will," she whispered, hesitantly reaching out to touch his arm lightly. He forced himself to stay still when she cringed slightly, but bravely kept her hand where it was. "Gypsy told me about you." Gypsy had told her sister about him? Slade felt his claws slowly begin to recede, along with his fangs as Sari went on, "She said you are the other half of her soul, and that if anyone ever took her, you would not stop until you found her."

"Gypsy explained mates to you?" Chase asked, the low growl in his voice demanding an answer. "She told you about shifters?" It was not necessarily forbidden to tell others about shifters, but it put the lives of many in danger.

"She did," Sari admitted, as she moved closer to Slade. "I already knew about shifters, but she said Slade would protect us because that's what mates do."

"She's right," Slade said, reaching out to gently pull the trembling girl to him. "I will keep you safe, and I will find your sister, no matter what it takes."

Chase's eyes narrowed on Sari, but he turned away, taking out his cell phone. "I'm going to try and contact Angel again."

"She can't help you right now," Jade interjected before he could place the call. "She is nowhere near here." Chase swore as he put his phone away, but Jade held up her hand. "Chase, you don't need Angel right now."

"Yes, I do, dammit," Chase growled in frustration. "I don't have the ability to find Gypsy quickly, Jade."

"No, but you have me," Jade replied, setting the chart she held on the counter and walking toward the door.

"Where are you going?" Chase demanded, following close behind.

"To gear up. I have a friend to find."

13

G ypsy came to slowly, her mind a jumbled, foggy mess. She could not seem to open her eyes, and no matter how hard she tried to get her arms and legs to cooperate, she was unable to move. Licking her lips, she groaned at the dry, cottony taste in her mouth. There was a dull ache in the back of her head, and her broken arm throbbed with pain. Her breath came in shallow pants, and Gypsy trembled in fear as she struggled to remember where she was.

The last thing she could recall was sitting with Sari in her hospital room. What had they been talking about? *Her magic, and shifters*, she thought. "Slade." Gypsy breathed his name quietly. She had told her sister about him, and what he was to her. An image of Sari sleeping seeped into her mind. She had decided it was time for her to go. After tucking her sister in, she'd left the hospital intending to go to Slade, but had stopped to take in the beauty of the night. Then, something sharp had pinched her neck, before total darkness overcame her.

"I see you are finally awake, my pet."

It was a voice from her past. One she had never thought she would ever hear again. *No!* She screamed the word silently, and it echoed in her mind. It was *him*! The monster of her nightmares...Titus. *Oh, God!* She had to get away from him. Struggling to open her eyes, Gypsy weakly moved her head. Her body shook with the need to jump and run, but her limbs were sluggish, and the most she could do was push up into a sitting position. Managing to open her eyes slightly, she cried out at the bright light that hit them. She heard his cruel laughter first, then he smacked her; a powerful blow across the face. "How dare you leave me, you bitch!" he yelled. "You are mine! I own you!"

Whimpering, Gypsy tried to scoot back away from him, crying out at the pain that shot up through her arm. Looking down in surprise, she saw that Titus had removed the cast.

"I broke your arm for a reason," he snarled. "I was teaching you a lesson. You obviously have more to learn, so you will suffer the way I originally intended."

Anger swamped her at his words. Cradling her broken arm to her chest, Gypsy hung her head, letting her long hair hide the defiance she knew was beginning to show on her face. She may be terrified of the man, but unlike her arm, *she* was not broken.

Hearing a loud, familiar clang, Gypsy stiffened, waiting until she heard the sound of heavy footsteps as Titus made his way up the stairs. Prying her eyes open, she got her first good look at her new prison. At first, she thought the son of a bitch had brought her back to The Dungeon, but she knew that was not possible. RARE had blown the place sky high when they rescued them. There was no Dungeon left, but this place was very similar. She only counted three cells this time, and she did not see a large table like the one they used to strap the prisoners to before, but there were several torture devices hanging from a piece of plywood screwed into the far wall. There was a steel chair in the center of the room bolted to the floor with what looked like metal cuffs that were used to clamp a prisoner's arms and legs to it. So, instead of a torture table, they had a torture chair. Did Titus think he was going to put her in it? No way in hell.

Struggling to her feet, Gypsy swayed as waves of darkness swarmed through her. *I will not faint!* she told herself. *I will not fall!* Stumbling to the front of the cell, she grasped the bars with her good hand. Leaning her head against cold metal, Gypsy closed her eyes and took a deep breath. She had no idea what Titus had drugged her with, but it was slowly starting to leave her system. She was beginning to feel her strength returning, and with it, the determination to find a way out of her prison. She had so much to live for, and she would fight to the end. She refused to ever become the weak, pitiful woman that bastard had made her before.

Gypsy knew Titus would not be gone long. He had brought her there for a reason, and torture was his favorite game. However, this time she vowed she would be the winner. She had gifts, powerful gifts, and she would use them.

Gypsy, can you hear me? The words whispered through her mind, so faint she almost missed them. *Gypsy? Please, answer me.*

Gypsy almost wept at the sound of Jade's voice. Of course, they would be looking for her! Slade would not stop until he found her, she knew it. *I'm here, Jade.*

Thank God! I've been trying to reach you for hours. Can you tell me where you are? Are you all right?

It depends on your definition of all right, Gypsy said wryly, looking down at her broken arm that she held against her waist. *I'm stuck in a basement that resembles the hell I just escaped, waiting on Titus to come back. I'm scared to death.*

Do you know where it is?

No. Titus drugged me when he took me. I just woke up a few minutes ago. He left, but he won't stay gone for long. He wants to punish me for leaving him.

Shit! Jade cursed, anger and fear in her voice. *We are going to find you, Gypsy. We are doing everything we can on our end right now.*

Gypsy's eyes narrowed on the torture toys across the room from her. While they were doing everything they could, she needed to do the same. No one was going to be there in time to save her. She was going to have to figure out a way to do it herself.

Concentrating on a large knife hanging on the wall, Gypsy shut out everything else around her, including the sound of Jade's voice. It had been so long since she had last tried to move anything with her mind because of the horrible pain she experienced afterwards, but she needed a weapon, and she needed it now. Taking a deep breath, she focused her gaze on the knife and willed it to come to her. When it didn't move, she tried again. After several failed attempts, she finally admitted defeat. Rubbing her forehead, she fought tears as she tried to figure out what to do next.

Maybe it's too big. Is there something smaller you can try?

Gypsy jumped at the sound of Jade's voice. She had almost forgotten about the other woman. Squinting, sharp stabs of pain shooting behind her eyes, she replied, *It looks like there is another knife smaller than the first, but I don't know how much damage it could do.*

Anything is better than nothing.

Jade was right. Even the smaller knife would be something to defend herself with. It would wound, even if it didn't kill. Gypsy breathed in deeply and slowly let it out. She did this several times, trying to calm her nerves. Holding her good arm out toward the wall, she narrowed her eyes on the weapon, trying to ignore the pounding in her temples. At first there was nothing, but then the knife began to tremble. Suddenly, Gypsy felt as if there was an added energy within her, something helping her, making her stronger. *Jade? Is that you?*

Yes. Concentrate, Gypsy!

Gritting her teeth, she willed the knife to come to her, watching in shock as it slowly slipped from the board and levitated across the room until it came to rest in her outstretched hand. Wrapping her fingers around the handle of the knife, she quickly slipped it into the back of her pants. *Now what?*

Now, you wait. The response was not what Gypsy wanted to hear, but there really wasn't anything else she could do. *You need to rest, Gypsy.*

I can't. He will be back soon. I have to be ready for him. She had no idea where Titus had gone, but there was no doubt in her mind that he would return to continue his game soon. She had seen the extreme possessiveness in his gaze. The desire to conquer her, and make her his. She would die before she let that happen.

Sit and rest. You will hear him when he comes, but if you don't rest, you will not be able to fight. What Jade said made sense, but Gypsy was scared to close her eyes.

I will be here, Gypsy. I promise, I won't leave you.

Gypsy hurt, she was exhausted, and she was terrified. She knew Jade was right. If she did not get some rest, she would be unable to defend herself. After one last look around the room, she walked over to the far corner of the cell and sat down with her back against the wall. The knife stayed hidden at her back, but within easy reach. It wasn't very big, about the size of your average steak knife, but it was something.

Allowing her eyes to slowly drift shut, Gypsy thought about Slade and their last words to each other. She had been upset that he had found someone to love and marry instead of waiting for her. A part of her had felt hurt and betrayed. Now she was just glad that he was able to experience love at least once in his life, because there was the very real possibility that she would not survive the next few hours.

Jade, if I don't make it out of here...

You WILL make it out of there, Gypsy Layne! Giving up is not an option.

I'm not giving up, Gypsy protested tiredly. *I just don't want to die without Slade knowing how I feel. I'm too weak to hold a connection with him. I need you to give him a message. Please.*

After a moment of silence, Jade whispered, *Tell me.*

Tears slipped down Gypsy's face as she collected her

thoughts. *Tell him that I understand what he was trying to tell me before. I was wrong to be upset, and I am so sorry that I left when I did. I never should have.* A ragged sob slipped out as she continued, *I hope I have the chance to someday earn his love myself. I want to spend the rest of my life showing him how much I...* before she could finish her sentence, the door at the top of the stairs groaned as it was opened, then it shut with a loud thud. *He's back, Jade.*

Gypsy scrambled to her feet, reaching back to make sure the knife was still there, even though she could feel the bite of the blade against her tender skin.

I'm not leaving you, Gypsy. I'm right here.

I can't help you hold our link. I don't have enough energy. It would take everything she had in her to defeat the monster walking down the stairs toward her, but losing was not an option. She wanted to go home to her family.

You don't have to. I'm strong enough to hold it for both of us. I will not leave you.

The raw determination in Jade's voice helped Gypsy shore up her courage. When Titus stopped in front of her cell, he would not see the terrified woman she had been back in The Dungeon. That woman was gone. In her place was one fighting for a future with her mate. Titus had no idea what he had awakened inside her. *You have to, Jade. You need to tell Slade what I told you. He needs to know that I love him, now and always.* Not waiting for a response, Gypsy severed their link.

———

SLADE STOOD in the corner of the conference room in Chase's office building, fighting his wolf, who wanted to take control and go find his mate. There was a flurry of activity as people came and went, doing what they could to help Gypsy. His best trackers were canvasing the area, looking for clues as to where Titus could have gone.

Becca had come to Chase the moment she heard Gypsy was taken to offer her computer skills. It would seem the woman was not only a brilliant scientist, but she was a computer genius as well. She sat at the table, her fingers flying over her laptop as she hunted for anything connected to Titus. So far, she had somehow managed to find out that his last name was Fendricks, he was ex-military, and he owned several properties all over the United States. He had no family to speak of, and no close friends.

Jade had tried several times to connect with Gypsy, but each attempt was unsuccessful. It meant one of two things; she was either unconscious or dead. Slade refused to believe the latter. Even though they had not completed the bond, he knew she was alive. He felt it.

Jade sat at the table, once again trying to reach Gypsy. Slade watched her intently, waiting for any sign that she was able to. A slight frown marred her features, and she was completely still, except for the clenching and unclenching of one hand. This time, she'd been silent longer than her previous attempts. He prayed that meant something…anything.

Slade blamed himself for everything that had happened since Gypsy left the day before. He never should have let her walk away from him. He should have followed her to the hospital and brought her back home. He should have told her that even though Sarah may have held his heart a century ago, she was not the one who held it now. There were so many things that he should have done differently, but he could not change the past. All he could do was hope for the chance to make it up to her in the future.

"Gypsy's in trouble." Slade jumped at the sound of Jade's voice.

Cursing softly at his lapse in concentration, he demanded, "You found her? What's going on? Is she hurt?"

"Titus has her, which we knew. She has no idea where she is, except it is similar to the place Perez held her and Trace. It's in a basement, much smaller than The Dungeon."

"Did he hurt her?" Slade demanded. He had to know that Gypsy was okay. He could not stand the thought of Titus touching her, inflicting pain on her.

Before Jade could respond, there was a commotion at the door and Bran walked in with the trackers. "That son of a bitch took her from the front steps of the hospital. We followed his scent a mile north where he cut a hole in the fence and slipped through. He must have had a vehicle waiting, because we lost his scent at the road."

"Who was patrolling the perimeter?" Even Slade had to fight not to shrink back at the fury in Chase's voice.

"We were," Kent said, as he and Tori stepped into the room. His body shook and he cowered in front of the alpha's anger. Slade's eyes narrowed and he snarled at the smell of recent sex that clung to the enforcers.

Chase stepped forward, a low growl emitting from his throat. "You were fucking when Slade's mate was stolen?"

A red haze of anger washed over Slade and when the change hit him, he did not fight it. Shifting quickly, he launched himself at Kent, attacking the man in blind rage.

The enforcer was no match for Slade, and soon he was on the ground, bleeding severely from several wounds.

"Enough!" The deep, commanding voice of his alpha was the only thing that stopped Slade from killing the other man. He wanted to tear out Kent's throat to show the others in the room what happened when anyone allowed his precious mate to be taken. His wolf growled in agreement, but Chase would not allow it.

"Let him go, Slade." Chase's tone brooked no argument, no matter how much Slade wanted to fight the command.

Loosening his jaw where it was currently wrapped around the enforcer's throat, Slade stepped back and growled in warning, before shifting. Baring his teeth, he snarled, "Gypsy is back in the hands of a psychopath who tortured her for months, a man I promised her I would keep her safe from, because you couldn't keep your dick in your pants while you were supposed to be ensuring the safety of not only my mate, but everyone in this compound."

When Tori stepped forward, Chase turned to her with a low growl. "You are both stripped of your enforcer titles, and will be placed in solitary confinement until I am ready to deal with you."

"But, Alpha…"

"No!" Chase's voice boomed throughout the small room. "You were under an oath to protect this pack. You broke that oath. Now go!"

As Kent struggled to rise, Tori shrank back toward the door. "Please," she whispered, "we didn't mean for any of this to happen."

Chase turned from her without another word. Bran

motioned to Sable and Charlotte, "Take them and lock them up."

"Slade," Becca called out from where she was still typing furiously into her keyboard. "I think I found something!"

Stalking over to a cupboard, Chase opened a door and removed a pair of jogging pants he kept there just in case something like this happened. When someone shifted with clothes on, it shredded them, leaving nothing but tatters. Throwing the pants to Slade, he said, "I will deal with Kent and Tori. You concentrate on Gypsy."

Slade slipped into them quickly, before moving to Becca's side. "Talk to me."

"I found six properties under the name Titus Fendricks. I was able to eliminate four of them because they do not have basements." Pointing to her computer screen, Becca said, "This one is all of the way across the states, but this one is just a six-hour drive from here. It matches the timeframe if he took her and drove straight there."

"That's exactly what he did!" Jade exclaimed, looking at the properties highlighted on the screen in front of her. "He would have to have a private jet or helicopter to fly her all of the way to New York. From what you found out, he doesn't own anything like that, and there's no way they would be there already if he drove."

"Figure out the fastest way to get there and send us the coordinates," Chase ordered Becca. "Slade, Bran, Jade, and I will go."

"We are going, too," Xavier said, stalking into the room. He was pale, but he moved easily, showing no outer sign of pain. He was dressed for battle, with his sidearm strapped to his leg, another on his hip, and a knife hooked to his belt. "Gypsy saved my life. Aiden and I are going to help save hers."

"I appreciate that, Xavier," Slade said, "but we can't have you slowing us down."

"Have I ever slowed you down before?" Xavier demanded. "I'm fucking going, whether it is with you, or on my own."

"The fastest route I can find will still take you approximately five and a half hours to drive," Becca interrupted. "I can't find anything quicker."

"I have a guy at the airport that owes me a favor," Bran said. "I'll get him to fly us there."

"I already checked, and the closest airport to where Gypsy is being held is just fifteen minutes away. I will make sure you have a vehicle waiting when you land," Becca promised.

"Good," Chase said shortly. "Get your gear, and let's get out of here. You have ten minutes to meet me out front."

Everyone left quickly, but Jade grabbed Slade's arm tightly before he could slip out of the conference room. She looked as if she were fighting an inner war before she finally said, "Slade, I promised Gypsy I would relay a message to you." Slade stiffened at the seriousness in her gaze. "She wants you to know that she understands why you chose to marry Sarah." Slade fought tears as Jade's eyes filled with compassion, "She said to tell you she loves you, and always will."

She loved him. Even after everything that had happened, Gypsy loved him. "I have to go," he growled, pulling his arm from Jade. He had to get out of there before he lost it. As Slade ran for his apartment to grab clothes and weapons, all he could think about was a pair of large, dark brown eyes full of sadness as they turned away from him. He had failed Gypsy once, but he would not do it again.

14

G ypsy's heart pounded in fear as she stared into the cold, heartless eyes returning her gaze, but she refused to show Titus the affect he had on her. Straightening her spine, she glared at him as she waited for him to speak.

Titus's mouth quirked up into an evil smirk as he reached down and cupped himself through his slacks. "You are finally mine to do with as I please. I've waited so long for this. I love to see the defiance in your eyes, my pet. It will be so much better if you fight me."

Gypsy froze as his meaning sank in. "Don't you dare touch me," she spat, fighting the urge to brandish the knife in front of her. She could not show her hand too soon, or she would never get the chance to shove the blade through his cold heart. Could she really do it? Could she take a life? The answer was yes. To protect herself, to live to spend another day with Slade and Sari, she would do whatever it took.

"Oh, I am going to do more than just touch you," Titus

said darkly, as he let go of himself to remove a key from his pocket. "I'm going to do many, many things to you." The cell door creaked open, and he stepped toward her. "Things you might not like now, but you will soon."

Gypsy held her ground, breathing harshly as terror raced through her. Just a little closer, she thought, reaching behind her back to grasp the handle of the knife. A couple more steps…that was all she needed.

"I am going to train you to obey my every command," Titus said, taking one more step toward her. "Before long, you will not only want my touch, you will crave it."

"Never," she hissed as he took the last step into her space. Swinging her arm around, she embedded the blade deep into his stomach, missing his heart by several inches.

"You fucking bitch," he yelled, grabbing her roughly and throwing her across the cell.

Gypsy cried out in pain as she fell to the floor, gasping when she landed on her broken arm. A wave of dizziness washed over her, and she fought to stay conscious. A hand grasped hold of her hair and yanked her to her feet, and she screamed when the back of Titus's hand connected with her cheek, dropping her to the ground once again. Bringing his foot back, he kicked her hard twice in the ribs. "Be ready, my pet," he ordered with one last kick, "After I fix this bloody mess you made, I will be back. You will learn who is boss!" Stalking out of the cell, Titus slammed the door shut before stomping up the stairs, shutting the lights off behind him.

Lying on the hard, cold cement floor, Gypsy clutched her useless arm to her aching ribs and cried. How had she let him get the better of her? She'd had the knife; the power. She should have at least been able to incapacitate him long enough to get away. Pain racked her body as she lay there afraid to move. Now what was she going to do? She had no weapon. She was defenseless.

It was so dark. Gypsy loved the night, but she had learned to hate the dark when she was unable to see the moon and the stars above. As she lay there, a sliver of light slipped through a small window on the back wall. She gasped as more came through another window on the wall above Titus's torture devices. The moon.

Gritting her teeth, Gypsy pushed herself up on her good arm. The light from the moon slowly made its way across the floor, until it stopped just inside her cell. Slowly, she began to drag herself toward her salvation, as ragged sobs were torn from her throat. It seemed to take forever, but soon she lay just in front of the cell door, her body bathed by the moonlight. Her eyes resting on the crest of the moon outside the window, she chanted softly,

Blessed Mother above,
Breathe your light into me,
Share with me your power,
Take my pain and suffering.

She repeated the words over and over, as tears of agony streamed down her face. The tingling started first in her fingers, spreading up her arms, over her shoulders, and then down her body. The glow around her became brighter and brighter, and she lay in shock as she felt her pain slowly starting to recede. It was working! Panting loudly, she rasped,

Blessed Mother above,
Breathe your light into me,
Share with me your power,
Your strength, and your energy.

Hearing the door at the top of the steps open, Gypsy lay still on the ground, waiting for Titus to come down the stairs. It didn't take long, and she continued chanting under her breath, even as he stood in front of her cell in shock.

"What the hell is wrong with you?" he demanded. When Gypsy didn't respond, he unlocked the door and yanked it open. Grasping her by her arms, he pulled her roughly to her feet in front of him.

Gypsy stared into his eyes as she chanted louder and louder. Waves of energy coursed through her broken body, building and building. When she felt as if she could not stand it anymore, she reached out and placed her right hand on Titus's chest, just over his heart. With everything she had, Gypsy shoved the energy from herself into Titus. It was like a huge bolt of electricity slamming into his chest, and he dropped her to the floor as it threw him across the room against his wall of toys.

Gypsy lifted her head weakly to look at the monster of her dreams, where he now lay on his back a mere twenty feet from her. His face was turned toward her, his eyes wide open in death, smoke rising from his body. Sighing, she lowered her head back to the floor as darkness swamped her.

15

Slade slowly crept around the outside of the old farmhouse, Jade right behind him. The place was creepy as hell, with old, rotted out boards falling off the side of it, several broken windows, and large holes in the roof. At least ten miles from the nearest town, out in the middle of nowhere, it was the perfect place to take someone if you did not want to be found.

Stopping at the corner of the house, Slade closed his eyes and inhaled deeply, wondering what the acrid smell was that seemed to be creeping up from the basement. Holding a hand up to Jade, he silently made his way to the window nearest to him and knelt down, peaking in. Unable to see clearly, he shook his head, rising and moving quickly to the front of the house. Just as he started up the front steps, Jade rushed past him. "Jade," he hissed, hurrying to keep up, "wait. You're going to put Gypsy in danger!"

Jade shook her head as she looked back. "There is only one person alive in this house, Slade, and it isn't Titus."

"What?"

Ignoring him, Jade entered the house and ran swiftly across what looked like the living room. "All clear!" Slade yelled as he followed. He made his way down a long hallway, gun drawn and ready.

"She's this way," Jade said quietly, as they entered the kitchen. "There!" The doorway to the basement was by the back porch, and soon he and Jade were both through it and running down the stairs. Before his eyes could adjust to the dark, someone up above flipped on the light switch, and Slade looked around in horror.

Titus lay dead on one side of the basement, staring sightlessly at them, and appearing as if he had been fried from the inside out. There were burn marks on the walls, and the ceiling was scorched. Slade realized that Titus had been what he had smelled outside. The stench of burnt flesh was overwhelming in the basement.

Gypsy was on the other side of the room, just inside a crudely made jail cell. She lay broken and bloody on the ground, appearing as if she, too, were dead.

She could not be gone. He would know if she was. He would know! "No," he moaned, crossing the floor to her and dropping to his knees. "Noooo!" Slade gathered Gypsy in his arms and rocked her back and forth, burying his face in her neck as screams of denial tore from his throat.

"Fuck me," Aiden whispered from the bottom of the stairs where he stood in shock.

Everyone watched in silence as Slade held his mate, praying she was alive, but wondering how anyone could live through something like that. It looked like a battle that no one had won.

"Slade," Jade said, gently touching his shoulder. He shrugged her off and clutched Gypsy tighter to him. "Slade, stop. You're going to hurt her."

That got his attention. Hurt her? She was dead, wasn't she? She lay limp in his arms, not moving. Pulling back, he looked at Jade in desperation. "She's alive?" he asked, daring to hope.

"Yes," Jade promised with a small smile. "Your mate lives, but we must get her back to Doc Josie quickly."

With shaky hands, Slade rested two fingers on the side of Gypsy's neck, relief hitting him when he felt a faint pulse. She was alive, but Jade was right. They needed to get her to Doc Josie. Holding her close, Slade stood, lifting her in his arms.

"Let's take her home," Chase said, clasping a hand on Slade's shoulder. Glancing over at Titus, he growled, "Make sure the bastard is dead, and then burn this place to the ground, with him in it."

———

TWENTY-FOUR HOURS LATER, Slade sat by Gypsy's bedside, her hand clasped tightly in his. The doctor had taped up her badly bruised ribs and reset her broken arm. She said Gypsy also suffered from a mild concussion, and that she would be very uncomfortable for days to come, but she would make a full recovery.

Sari sat curled up in a chair in the corner, sound asleep. She had refused to leave her sister's side since they returned. Slade understood, because he had not left Gypsy, either. He needed to be there when she woke up.

He wanted to be the first thing she saw, so she would know she was safe.

Slade reached out and lightly traced a finger down the side of her badly bruised and battered face. Gypsy had been through so much in the past year. She had gone through the unimaginable and survived. She was strong and courageous, and he was so proud to call her his. Leaning forward, he whispered softly, "Come back to me, baby. I need you." Resting his head on their hands, he closed his eyes.

He wasn't sure how long he sat like that before he felt the slight movement against his fingertips. Raising his head, he whispered Gypsy's name just as her eyes fluttered open. Slowly, she looked around the room and then back at him in confusion. "Slade?"

"I'm here," he rasped, fighting tears. "I'm right here, and you're safe, Gypsy." Cupping her cheek in his palm, he bent down to kiss her gently on the lips. "We're back at the compound."

"Titus?" she asked softly.

"He's gone, Gypsy. You never have to worry about him again." He expected to see relief in her eyes, but instead saw horror and self-condemnation. "Gypsy…"

"I killed him," she whispered raggedly, trying to tug her hand from his. "I'm a murderer."

"No," Slade growled, "you are a *survivor*, Gypsy Layne. A fucking *survivor*, and I am so proud of you."

Gypsy's lower lip trembled and her eyes filled with tears. "I told myself I would do whatever I had to do to get back to you and Sari. But, Slade, I took a life!"

Sliding onto the bed beside Gypsy, Slade wrapped her in his arms carefully, holding her close. He didn't know what to say to make her feel better. He would have killed the bastard himself in a heartbeat and saved her the guilt if he could have. Nuzzling the top of her head with his chin, he rasped, "I was so scared when I found out Titus had taken you." When she didn't respond, he whispered, "I was afraid I would never see you again, never get to hold you and tell you how much you mean to me."

Gypsy stilled, pulling back slightly to look up at him. "Me, too. Did Jade tell you what I told her to?" she asked quietly.

Cupping her cheek in the palm of his hand, he looked her in the eyes as he said, "I wish I could tell you that I would have done things differently over a hundred years ago if I had known you were coming to me someday, Gypsy. But, I honestly can't say that. I loved Sarah, and I was happy with her. I am grateful for the time we got together. Losing her and my child was devastating."

"Oh my God, Slade," Gypsy gasped, covering his hands with hers. "I didn't know you lost a child, too. I am so sorry!"

"I lost them both in childbirth," he told her roughly. Leaning his forehead against hers, he whispered, "I want to tell you I'm sorry I didn't wait for you, Gypsy, but I will never lie to you. What I will tell you, though, is that you are the light to my darkness. You have brightened my world since you came into my life, and you make me feel things that I haven't felt in a century. I want to be your mate, in every sense of the word, if you will have me. I will spend the rest of our lives doing everything in my power to keep you safe and make you happy."

A tremulous smile crossed Gypsy's lips, her eyes shining with emotion. "I want that, too, Slade."

"Good." Kissing her softly, he said, "I want to do this right. I want to have a mating ceremony soon, so that we can pledge our lives together in front of the pack."

"Okay," Gypsy agreed softly, "When?"

"Not for a couple of weeks, at least," Doc Josie said from the doorway. "You need to be stronger to handle the shift."

Slade didn't want to wait, but he knew the doctor was right. After everything Gypsy had gone through, she needed time to heal. Then her words sank in. Why hadn't he thought about the fact that Gypsy was human? Going through the change would be hell on her small body.

"Shift?" Gypsy asked, lying back against the pillow to look at Doc Josie. "What do you mean?"

"After the mating ceremony takes place, you and Slade will need to consummate the mating and exchange bites. That's what will bind you together for all eternity." Walking in to stand by the bed, the doctor smiled down at Gypsy. "Mates are not meant to live apart. When Slade bites you, you will become like us. You will have the power to shift into a wolf, and you may live hundreds of years."

Gypsy's eyes widened, "Hundreds of years?" she croaked.

Josie laughed, "I think the longest I have ever heard a shifter living was just over five hundred years. He passed on when his last child was killed around fifty years ago." Opening up the chart in her hand, she said, "I'm glad you are awake, Gypsy. I have some questions that I am hoping you can answer for me."

Slade felt Gypsy stiffen as she watched the doctor

closely, but she nodded, clutching tightly to his hand. "I think I know what you are going to ask me."

Raising an eyebrow, Doc Josie questioned mildly, "And your answer is?"

"Magic," Gypsy said simply. "I think that is something you can understand."

After a moment of silence, the doctor shut her chart and nodded thoughtfully. "Yes, it most definitely is." Tapping her finger to her chin, she continued, "With the rapid rate you are healing at right now, I would say a mating ceremony would be fine on the next full moon, which is two and a half weeks from today. If you want to set the date with the alpha, Slade, I will let him know that Gypsy will be fine by then."

Slade looked worriedly at Gypsy, so tiny and fragile in the hospital bed. "Are you sure she will be strong enough by then?"

"I guarantee it," Josie said with a wink, laughing as she left the room.

"Slade?" He turned back to Gypsy, his frown still in place. He knew she was strong, she had proven herself over and over again, but she had been through so much. He didn't want to cause her more pain. "Slade," she whispered again. "Please, stop worrying. I will be fine. I want to do this."

Leaning in to give her another soft, sweet kiss, he responded, "I know, sweetheart. I just…"

Gypsy silenced him with another kiss. "I am going through with that ceremony. Besides, you forget one thing."

"What?"

"I have magic on my side." He could not help returning

her smile. She was so beautiful, even with the bruises marring her delicate skin, and she was his.

Gypsy grasped the blanket covering her, pulling it aside. Slipping her legs over the side of the bed, she started to rise.

"What are you doing?"

Her eyes warmed as she reached up to run a hand over his dark hair. "Going home."

16

The next couple of weeks flew by for Gypsy. The days were spent at the hospital with her sister, the nights in Slade's arms. However, even though he held her close through the night, he refused to take it any further than kisses and light touching. He said it was hard enough to wait to claim her, and he was afraid he would not be able to control his wolf once he was deep inside of her. Slade wanted everything to be perfect, and to him, that meant waiting for the mating ceremony. So, instead, they spent their nights talking and sharing bits and pieces of their lives with one another. She told him about her life before her kidnapping, and he told her about Sarah and his struggle after her death. Each day, Gypsy felt herself falling more and more in love with Slade, but she was still waiting for him to say those three little words to her. She would wait forever if she had to. Her love was strong enough for both of them.

Gypsy also spent time with Jade, talking not only

about her time in The Dungeon, but also about Titus and the suffering he put her through. She was finally coming to terms with his death, and her part in it. She would never forget what she had done, but she was beginning to accept it and move on.

Sari had elected to stay at the hospital for now, even though Slade had offered her the spare bedroom in his apartment. She said she felt safer in the building surrounded by people she was now getting to know, and she wanted to have Doc Josie and Jade near.

The night of the ceremony was beautiful, the sky full of stars. The moon was slowly peeking around the clouds, and would be in full view soon. The White River wolf pack had gathered outside their alpha's home to witness Slade and Gypsy's mating. The only thing missing right now was Slade's mate.

Clutching the long, silky white gown in her hands, Gypsy ran swiftly up the hospital steps, through the front doors, and down the hall. Skidding to a stop in front of her sister's room, she gasped when Sari turned to her, a vision in light blue. Holding her arms out, Sari asked, "How do I look?"

Smiling, Gypsy crossed the room and hugged her sister to her. "Like a princess," she whispered.

Sari giggled, a sound Gypsy had been afraid she would never hear from the girl again. "You are the princess, Gypsy! And you need to go marry your prince!"

Stepping back, Gypsy laced her fingers with Sari's. "Let's go."

They left the room together, but Gypsy stopped when she heard a noise down at the very end of the hall. Turning, she saw Jade slip into a room, shutting the door quietly behind her. Curious, she let go of Sari's hand and made her way down the hall. She knew there was a patient in that room, but had never asked who it was.

Grasping the handle, Gypsy slowly opened the door and looked inside. A beautiful woman with long, black hair and toffee colored skin lay in the bed, a serene expression on her face. Jade sat by her side, head bowed. Not wanting to disturb them, but feeling as if she might somehow be able to help, Gypsy hesitated before stepping inside and letting the door shut behind her. "Jade?"

A shudder ran through Jade before she responded, "This is Rikki. She is my mentor, my friend." Wiping tears from her eyes, she whispered, "I think she's dying, Gypsy. She's been like this for weeks now, showing no sign of life. I can't reach her. I don't know what to do."

Gypsy's eyes narrowed as she stared at the woman on the bed. "What happened to her?"

"After we rescued you from Perez, we found out he had gone after Trace's mother and sister." Jade's voice caught as she went on, "Rikki was almost killed when we went to save them. My father told Jinx and me one time that mates aren't the only ones who can change someone with a bite. Strong alphas possess the power as well. It was Rikki's only chance of survival, so Jinx had Angel change her."

"So, she is like you now? A wolf?"

"Yes," Jade replied, reaching out to take Rikki's hand in hers. "I can smell the wolf in her. It worked. But she has never woken up. She doesn't respond to any of us. I have tried to connect with her, but there's just nothing."

"She isn't dying, Jade." Gypsy walked around to the other side of the bed and rested one hand on Rikki's forehead and one on her chest. "I can sense death, and there is none here." Closing her eyes, she slowly merged with Rikki, not surprised at what she found. The young woman was lost and alone. She was both frightened and angry; frightened because she had no idea how to find her way back to the land of the living, and angry because it made her feel weak, and she hated nothing more than feeling powerless. But, there was also a part of her that was not ready to wake up and face life again. That part was what really kept her from returning.

Let me help you, Gypsy whispered. *Let me bring you home.* There was no response. *Please, Rikki. Your friends are worried about you. They miss you.* But there was still no response. Gypsy tried several more times to get Rikki's attention, but nothing seemed to work. Sighing, she slipped back out of Rikki's mind, removing her hands from the other woman's body.

"Gypsy?"

"I'm sorry, Jade," Gypsy said, as she reached out and ran a hand down Rikki's beautiful hair. "I'm not sure what to do. My experience is with people near death. Your friend is very much alive. She is just lost and confused, and for some reason she can't seem to hear me."

"She's all right, though?" Jade asked hopefully. "She's alive and well?"

"Yes," Gypsy agreed, "but I don't know for how long. I've never dealt with anything like this before. I need to do some research."

"You'll help me?"

"Of course, I will help you," Gypsy promised, walking

over to Jade and hugging her close. "After everything you have done for me, Jade, there isn't anything I wouldn't do for you." Not only had Jade been there for her when she needed help getting through all of her trials and tribulations, but she had become a good friend. Gypsy didn't have many of them anymore, and she valued the friendships she was making.

"I'm sorry to interrupt, but we should probably get going, Gypsy. Slade's probably wondering where we are."

Her sister's tentative voice from the doorway brought them apart, and Gypsy gasped as she realized she was late for her own mating ceremony. "Oh, no! I have to go!"

Jade rose, before bending over to give Rikki a gentle kiss on the brow. "Come back to us soon, my friend." Grabbing Gypsy's hand, she said, "I think you have kept Slade waiting long enough. Let's go before he comes looking for you."

Gypsy giggled, but then looked back at Rikki. "You should stay with her, Jade."

"Let me ask you something, Gypsy. Do you honestly think there is any chance Rikki will wake up while I am gone tonight?"

Glancing at the window, Gypsy shook her head. "Maybe with the full moon, but I doubt it. She is lost, but she isn't really ready to return. I'm not sure why, but I promise you, I will find out."

Jade nodded, squeezing Gypsy's hand. "Then let's go. I want to be there for you. I've never experienced a mating ceremony." Smiling, she whispered, "You are absolutely beautiful, Gypsy."

Gypsy looked down at the ankle-length, white dress she wore. It had long fitted sleeves covered in lace, a low-cut bodice that cupped her breasts, tapering down to her slim waist and flaring out afterwards, the filmy material flowing as she walked. She had never owned anything so lovely, and could not wait to see the look in Slade's eyes when he saw her. Josie had come by earlier and curled her hair, pulling it back away from her face, but allowing it to spill down her back in waves. She had also helped with her makeup, and had given her turquoise earrings and a matching necklace as a mating gift.

"Are you ready?" Sari asked softly.

Turning to her sister, Gypsy took a deep breath. "More than ready."

They arrived at Chase's house less than five minutes later, and a hush fell over the pack as Gypsy glided across the lawn to stand beside Slade in front of the alpha.

"Everything all right?" Slade asked quietly, reaching out to enfold her hand in his. His eyes were full of concern, and something else. Happiness, desire...love?

Hope building in her chest, Gypsy nodded, taking a step closer to him. "It is now."

They both turned back to Chase, kneeling before him. Gypsy lowered her gaze, tensing slightly when she felt the touch of Chase's hand as he rested it lightly on the top of her head. "Slade Dawson and Gypsy Layne come before us for two reasons." Chase's voice rang out powerful and clear, and the slight push of his alpha energy toward her calmed Gypsy, allowing her to listen intently. Slade had explained to her exactly what would be expected at the gathering, but she was still nervous. "Tonight, not only do we celebrate the addition of a new member to our pack, but we will also celebrate a mating!"

Excitement stirred among the pack, and several

cheered loudly. Slade squeezed her hand lightly, and she closed her eyes, soaking in his nearness.

"Gypsy Layne, do you accept me as your alpha? Your leader?"

"Yes, I do." She spoke with pride and confidence.

"Do you accept the White River Wolf Pack as your own?"

"Yes, Alpha, I do."

"And do all of you accept Gypsy as pack?" His voice boomed over the gathering, and Gypsy smiled as cheers rose from the crowd.

Gypsy felt a push of energy flow from Chase into her. Gasping, her eyes rose to meet his. The power he invoked was unbelievable. Chase returned her gaze, a small smile forming on his lips. "Welcome to the pack, Gypsy." Raising his gaze from hers, he held out his hand to someone behind her. Turning, she saw Sari standing near Jade, a look of longing on her face. Sari slowly walked forward and slipped her hand in his, kneeling in front of him. "Sari Layne," his words were softer this time, more gentle. "Do you accept me as your alpha? Do you accept the White River Wolf Pack as your own?"

A soft sob caught in Sari's throat, as she nodded. "Yes, Alpha. Yes, I do."

Once again, Chase asked his pack for approval, and it was immediately given. Gypsy's heart filled with love for each and every one of them. They had accepted not only her, but also her sister, as a part of them. She and Sari had a family again.

Gypsy watched as Chase's sister, Jenna, appeared next to him and passed him a ceremonial knife. Slade had told her this was a very important part of the ritual. This was what would bind her to the pack. Holding her head high, she extended her hand to him, waiting while Chase made a small cut on the palm of her hand. Afterwards, he did the same to himself. Clasping their hands together so their blood merged, Chase's voice once again rang out over the crowded area. "You are now pack, bound by blood." After repeating the process with Sari, he pulled the young girl to her feet, hugging her gently. "Go back with Jade now, child."

Sari looked at Gypsy, her eyes bright with hope and unshed tears. Gypsy wasn't sure if it was allowed or not, but she rose and wrapped her arms around her sister, holding her for a moment before letting her go. "I love you, Sari," she whispered softly.

"Me, too." Sari's response was so quiet, Gypsy almost missed it. She knew her sister was feeling overwhelmed with everything, so she let her go without another word. Turning back to Chase, she once again knelt beside Slade, slipping her hand back in his, and waited to see what would happen next.

She sighed as Chase rested his hand on her head, pushing more of his alpha power her way. It strengthened her and made her feel safe. It was a gift, one she would always cherish. "Today we not only welcome two new members to the pack, but we also celebrate a union between Slade and Gypsy. As you all know, the great spirits bless us with one mate, and one mate only. When they do, they bind our souls together, making us one. Not everyone finds the other half of their soul, but Slade and Gypsy have. As alpha of this pack, I ask the spirits to bind them tonight, for all eternity."

Gypsy wasn't sure exactly what she expected, but it

was not the bright glow that emanated from their clasped hands, to slowly spread out and engulf their bodies. Soon, she and Slade glowed brightly, to the astonishment of the pack. Grinning, Gypsy leaned her head back and looked up at the full moon above. "She gives her blessing as well."

17

W hen the ceremony was over, and everyone had left, Gypsy and Slade said goodbye to Chase and slowly made their way back home. Since it was a full moon, the chance of Gypsy shifting that night after Slade bit her was high, so Chase said to call him as soon as the change started. Having her alpha there to help her through the painful process would make it much easier on her.

They barely made it inside the front door, before Slade slammed it shut and pulled her into his arms. "Mine," he growled, covering her mouth with his. He had waited so long to be inside her again. He couldn't wait anymore. He needed to touch her, to feel her skin against his. "This first time is going to be fast, Gypsy. I'm sorry, I can't wait."

Gypsy grabbed hold of his white-button down shirt and yanked it open, ripping the buttons down the front. "I don't need slow," she told him. "I need you."

A low growl rumbled in Slade's chest as he backed Gypsy up against the wall, before kicking off his shoes and then undoing his dress slacks and letting them fall to the floor. Sliding his hands under her dress, he ran them up her thighs to the silk panties she wore. Tearing them from her, Slade grasped her legs and lifted her up, turning and walking into the dining room to set her on the kitchen table. Never taking his eyes from hers, he pushed her dress up over her waist and spread her legs wide.

Pulling Gypsy so her hips rested just off the table, Slade grasped his aching cock and slid it inside her. *Fuck*, she was so hot and sweet. Holding onto her hips, he started to move, savoring the feel of her tightening around his dick with each thrust.

Slade. The sound of her voice inside his head drove him wild. The sexy rasp had his cock hardening even more, and his fangs dropped as he thrust deep inside her. Her head was flung back, and her neck and shoulders were bare, calling to him.

Grasping her tighter, Slade snarled as he fought for control. His hips moved faster and faster, the desire to claim her pushing him on. Knowing he was getting close, he slipped an arm around Gypsy's waist and pulled her up until he could easily reach her shoulder. This time he didn't hesitate. Opening his mouth, he sank his teeth into her skin, roaring as she came around him, pushing him over the edge. Sliding a hand through her hair, he guided her mouth to his shoulders, groaning when he felt her small, blunt teeth return his bite. They were human teeth, and just barely broke the skin, but it was enough. He felt the bond click into place, joining them as one. She was his now, forever.

And you are mine.

After several minutes, Slade picked Gypsy up and

carried her to bed. Sliding her dress off, he hung it up in the closet. When he returned, she had fallen asleep. Climbing into bed beside her, he snuggled her close, kissing her gently on the cheek, before allowing himself to follow her into sleep.

GYPSY WOKE AN HOUR LATER, stretching languidly as she thought about Slade. A soft smile covered her lips as she remembered the look in his eyes when he saw her at the ceremony. He cared for her. It may not be love just yet, but she held out hope that it would be some day.

"What are you thinking about?"

She jumped at the sound of Slade's voice near her. Opening her eyes, she grinned at him, saying teasingly, "I was just wondering what I have to do to get you to bite me again."

Slade's eyes darkened, and he growled, "Just ask."

Reaching out, Gypsy ran a hand through his thick hair, down his neck to his chest. Rising to her knees, she pushed him back against the bed and leaned down to place a trail of kisses down his hard chest. "Gypsy," Slade gasped, tangling his hands in her hair.

"Yes," she breathed, nipping his skin just above his belly button, then soothing it with her tongue. Feeling his hard cock brush against her breast, she looked up at him and smiled. *Mine,* she told him, reiterating what he had kept telling her not too long ago.

Yours, he agreed, his eyes flaring wide with desire.

Sliding down the bed until her mouth was right over his cock, Gypsy slowly licked it from the base to the tip, before encircling the head with her tongue. Savoring the salty pre-cum taste, she sucked him inside, taking him in as far as she could. Cupping his balls in her hand, she rolled them in her palm, and then tugged gently.

"Gypsy!" Slade yelled, jerking his hips and pushing his dick deeper into her mouth.

Sliding her hands under him, Gypsy cupped his firm ass. Digging her nails in slightly, she began to slowly move up and down on his cock, sucking him deeper and deeper in each time. Suddenly, Slade's hands tightened in her hair and he took over, thrusting faster, but careful not to hurt her.

Just when she thought he was getting close, Slade pulled out of her mouth with a snarl. Looking up at him, she froze when she met the eyes of his wolf. His fangs had dropped, and his claws were starting to emerge.

Sitting up, Slade pulled Gypsy forward and placed her hands on the headboard. Positioning himself behind her, he grasped her hips and slowly slid his thick cock deep inside her. Gypsy flung her head back, holding onto the bed as she pushed back against him, begging him to move.

Slade pulled out, and then pushed back in as deep as he could, again and again. She met him thrust for thrust. Letting go of Gypsy's hips, Slade slipped his hands around and cupped her full breasts, bringing her back against his chest. She cried out as he pinched her nipples, then flicked them with his thumbs. She was so damn close.

One of Slade's hands left her breast to move down her stomach. "Oh, God!" Slade thrust deep as he found her clit and began to rub it. "Slade, please! Bite me!"

She needed to feel him claim her again. Needed to know that she was his. Reaching behind her, she slid her hands into Slade's hair, urging him to her shoulder. Slade licked her once, then twice, before sinking his teeth deep. Gypsy screamed as she came, Slade quickly following.

Slade held Gypsy close for several minutes before finally sliding out of her. Removing his teeth, he licked his mating bite, sending a shiver running down her spine. "We are bonded together now," he said quietly. "No matter what."

Turning to face him, Gypsy cradled his face in her hands. "I love you, Slade Dawson." When he would have responded, she covered his mouth with her thumbs, a loving smile on her lips. "It's okay. I understand. Just know this, I will never ask you to forget about Sarah and your child. They are a part of you, and should always remain in your heart. I just pray that someday, you will find room in there for me, too."

Gathering her up in his arms, Slade rose from the bed and walked over to a large chair that set in the corner of the room. Sitting down, he placed her on his lap, holding her close. "Gypsy, you are right. A part of me will always love Sarah. I won't deny it. But, my heart belongs to you now." Gypsy's eyes widened in shock and hope as he continued, "You mean everything to me, my love. I live for you, and I would die for you. We are one."

"Slade," she whispered, fighting tears of joy that threatened slip free, "I love you so much."

Kissing her gently, Slade said, "I have a present for you, sweetheart." Reaching around her, he opened the top drawer in the dresser by the chair. "You have talked about this several times in the past few weeks, so I sent Charlotte and Sable to your old home to see if they could find it." Retrieving an old, thick book, he placed it in her hands. "I'm sorry, the place was burned to the ground, but they were able to retrieve this from where you had kept it hidden in the old cellar."

Tears streamed unchecked down Gypsy's cheeks as she held her father's book tightly. With just that one gesture, sending his enforcers all of the way across several states to find something so precious, he had proven his love to her. Leaning her head against his chest, she sobbed. "My parents?" She knew they were dead. Not only had she been forced to watch Perez's men kill them, but she had felt death come and take them from her while she was unable to help. However, she had no idea what had been done with their bodies.

"Sable was able to find out where they were buried, and Chase has started proceedings to have their bodies exhumed and moved to a cemetery close by where we bury our own."

"Thank you, Slade," she whispered. "Thank you. You don't know what this means to me."

"I would do anything for you, Gypsy," Slade replied, wiping her tears away. "You are the most important person in my life." Kissing her softly, he said, "I have one more surprise for you."

"But you have done so much already!"

"I will always do everything I can to make you happy," he responded, nuzzling her cheek with his own. "I talked to Chase, and I told him that we either need a bigger apartment or a house. I know you would like Sari to come live with us, and this apartment just isn't big enough for three. I also know that Sari is scared to be alone because of everything that happened. So what we worked out, if it is all right with you, is we are going to build a three-bedroom home near Phoenix and Serenity's place. We will put in a state of the art security system, and Sari will not only have us, but she will have a member of RARE living next door. I think she will feel safe enough to leave the hospital then."

"That sounds so wonderful," Gypsy whispered, hearing only half of what he was saying. Sharp stabs of pain had started shooting through her body, subtle at first, but growing more painful with every second. Sweat beaded up on her forehead, and her vision started to blur. "Slade," she gasped, finally interrupting him as he talked about their new place. "Call Chase!"

Suddenly the pain was overbearing, feeling as if it were tearing her apart from the inside out. Slade quickly stood and ran to the bed, placing her gently on it. She was aware of him placing a call to Chase, before he left the room for a moment. Soon he was back by her side, applying a cool washcloth to her forehead.

"Slade!" She screamed his name as she curled up into a fetal position on the bed, holding her knees tightly to her chest. A thin sheen of sweat coated her body, and she moaned as another wave of pain slammed through her. "Slade," she screamed again.

"I'm right here, baby."

Suddenly, a light seemed to push through the curtains, making its way toward her. *The moon,* she whispered to Slade, hoping he would understand.

18

Slade stared down at Gypsy in horror and fear as her muscles contracted and she screamed in torment. He was aware of Chase rushing into the room and immediately going to Gypsy's side to place a hand on her back. He knew his alpha was sharing some of his power with Gypsy, trying to stave off some of the pain she was feeling. He recoiled as her screams pierced the air, taken back to a time years ago when another woman he loved died from experiencing pain and suffering because of him. If he had not gotten her pregnant, she would have lived. If he had not bitten Gypsy, she would not be going through hell right now. It was all his fault.

Stop it! Dammit, Slade, stop it right now. I need you! Gypsy's anger finally broke through his panic and dread. *Open the curtain.*

Slade stared at her in confusion for a moment, before he realized what she meant. Running to the window, he quickly tore the curtain down off the rod, letting the light of the moon stream in and cover Gypsy. As he watched, she immediately began to calm, her screams lessening and her breathing becoming less labored. Then, the change began to take place. Since it was her first shift, it took longer than normal, but soon a beautiful dark brown wolf lay where Gypsy's naked body had been just moments before.

Chase ran a hand over Gypsy's coat, crooning softly to her. "You did good, little one. Very good. Tomorrow night, we will take a run together; you, Slade, and me. But right now, I think you may have other things on your mind."

"Thank you, Alpha," Slade rasped, as Chase stood to leave, never taking his eyes off Gypsy.

Chase walked over to Slade and clasped him on the shoulder, "Congratulations, Slade. You have a fine mate." Turning to leave, he said, "I'm giving you a few days off. You've earned it. Spend time with Gypsy, strengthen your bond. Love each other." Chase left the room without another word, and it wasn't long before Slade heard the front door shut quietly.

Slade's wolf was pushing at him to change. He wanted to run with his mate. "Come on," he said, motioning to the door. "Let's get out of here." Gypsy rose, shaking out her dark coat. She took one tentative step to the side of the bed, then another, before jumping lightly to the floor. As soon as they were out of the apartment, Slade shifted, immediately rubbing against Gypsy to mark her with his scent. She pulled away from him and took off down the street and out of town. Howling loudly, he ran after her, following her across the large open land and through the trees beyond.

They ran for a couple of miles before Gypsy finally

came to a stop. Slade watched in awe as she transformed from her wolf into the amazing beauty he had fallen in love with. Quickly shifting himself, he opened his arms and she walked into them. "I love you, Gypsy Layne."

Leaning back to look at him, Gypsy grinned through her fangs. "I love you too, my mate."

His cock hardened instantly when he realized what she had planned. Picking her up, he braced her back against the smooth bark of a tree, making sure it wasn't biting into her tender flesh, before sliding deep inside her and beginning to move. Finding his mate mark, he began to lightly lick and suck on it until he knew she was ready, and then he bit down. He came on a roar as she returned his bite, her fangs sinking deep, claiming him as he had her. They were one, for all eternity.

Make sure and visit my website for information on all of my books, and to sign up for my Newsletter where you will receive all of the latest information on new releases, sales, and more!

Website: **http://www.dawnsullivanauthor.com/**

I would love to have you join my reader's group, Author Dawn Sullivan's RARE Rebels, so that we can hang out and chat, and where you will also get sneak peeks of cover reveals, read excerpts before anyone else, and more!

https://www.facebook.com/groups/AuthorDawnSullivan sRebelReaders/

Dawn Sullivan

ABOUT THE AUTHOR

Dawn Sullivan has a wonderful, supportive husband, and three beautiful children. She enjoys spending time with them, which normally involves some baseball, shooting hoops, taking walks, watching movies, and reading.

Her passion for reading began at a very young age and only grew over time. Whether she was bringing home a book from the library, or sneaking one of her mother's romance novels to read by the light in the hallway when she was supposed to be sleeping, Dawn always had a book. She reads several different genres and subgenres, but Paranormal Romance and Romantic Suspense are her favorites.

Dawn has always made up stories of her own, and finally decided to start sharing them with others. She hopes everyone enjoys reading them as much as she enjoys writing them.

facebook.com/dawnsullivanauthor

twitter.com/dawn_author

instagram.com/dawn_sullivan_author